Blame It On
The Candy Canes

Samantha Baca

Sugarplum Falls Series

Blame It On The Mistletoe

Blame It On The Eggnog

Blame It On The Candy Canes

Blame It On The Reindeer

Blame It On The Carols

Blame It On The Blizzard

Cover Design: Richard Baca
Image (s): DepositPhotos

Contents

<u>One</u>
Andi

"You have to kiss me!" I blurted out as I burst into the kitchen area, startling Zach as he put the final touches on a custom cake we were working on for a holiday party.

"What?" he asked, laughing as he set the icing bag down and turned toward me. "What are you talking about?" His icy blue eyes glistened in the light with amusement at my outburst.

"My parents are coming to Sugarplum Falls for Christmas. But they decided at the last minute to change their plans and come in early so they could make their friends' holiday party. My mom just called, and they're on their way here. She already mentioned me going with them to the party, which I just know is a ploy to try to set me up with her friend's son. I've met him, and he's horrible."

"Okay, so how do I come into play in all this?" He crossed his ankles as he leaned against the counter behind him and watched me with curiosity.

"I *might* have told them I was dating someone and had plans to go to my *boyfriend's* family holiday party instead."

"So, again, how does this involve me kissing you?"

"Because," I sighed and tipped my head back, not having the courage to look him in the eyes as I said it. "I told them *you* are my boyfriend. They're on their way here to check out my *cute little shop* and meet my new boyfriend."

The sound of his laughter echoing off the walls made me open my eyes and glare at him.

"This isn't funny! I'm in a real bind here!"

"Okay, okay, I'm sorry. It's not funny."

My face softened for a split second until I saw the smirk gracing his lips. I reached over and swatted his shoulder with a dish towel.

I was about to say something else but heard the bells chime up front as the door opened. I paused and listened, even though I already knew who it was. It was busy and could have been *any* customer, but fate was messing with me right now, and I knew it was my parents.

"Shit!" I whispered, covering my mouth.

"Hi, we're here to see Andi. We're her parents," my dad explained to Becky, who was working the register.

"Oh, how nice to meet you. Let me grab her for you. She's in the back."

I strained to listen to their conversation, tilting my head to the side while Zach grinned like a fool. I knew he found this funny, but I was a nervous wreck as it wasn't like me to lie to my parents—ever.

"If it's okay, can we go back instead? We were hoping to surprise her."

I rolled my eyes, knowing damn well that they were not *hoping to surprise me*, given that I had just gotten off the phone with my mom a few minutes ago and she said they were on their way.

My eyes pinched shut, and I tried not to panic as I heard heavy footsteps approaching. Thankfully, they hadn't seen us through the window that opened the kitchen to the front of the store.

Before I could process what was happening, Zach grabbed my wrist and pulled me into him as his arms wrapped around my waist. My hands planted firmly against his chest as I tried to catch myself.

I looked up at him while my heart beat wildly in my chest. He smelled good. Had I ever noticed before how delicious he smelled? It was like the perfect blend of masculine cologne mixed with the sweet scent of sugar and baked goods.

He winked before lowering his lips to mine. I gasped softly as I felt the warm, soft touch as they feathered over my mouth, teasing me with a gentle nip here and there. I parted my lips, allowing him access as his tongue eagerly explored. My hands gripped the back of his head, ensuring he didn't stop.

He bent me back slightly—the way they do in the movies where the woman is knocked off her feet by the romantic hero sweeping in to save her from whatever she needs saving from. Anyway, long story short, he gave me *the dip* and then continued to kiss me like no one was watching, even though we heard the very loud gasp from my parents as they walked into the kitchen.

"Andi!" my mom exclaimed, her tone sharp enough to bring me upright before Zach pulled away and discreetly wiped his lips while fighting another grin. Thankfully, no one else was in the back with us because that would have been pretty difficult to explain.

"Mom! Dad!" I spun around, my cheeks flushed with embarrassment as well as some heat from the way Zach had just kissed me. *Who knew he had that in him?* "Sorry, I wasn't expecting you so soon," I lied.

"Well, I told you we were on our way," my mother replied, her arms crossed over her chest.

"Yeah. Right. Sorry. I um…"

"I'm sure Andi expected it to be longer due to the reindeer issue on Main Street."

"Reindeer issue?" my father questioned, eyebrow raised.

"Yes, sir. One of the reindeer escaped their pen this morning. It was a wild goose chase as the town gathered to try to capture him, and unfortunately, it stalled traffic for quite a while. Last I heard, they still had Main Street blocked off while they waited for him to come out of hiding."

"Oh, well. There seems to be quite the entertainment here in Sugarplum Falls," my father noted.

"Andi?" my mom whispered, widening her eyes as she looked pointedly at Zach.

My brain was fried, a complete scrambled mess as I tried to pick up on the cryptic clue she was giving me. Then it suddenly clicked, and I knew what she was talking about.

"Thank you for your help, Zach. Now, if you don't mind, we need to get that cake finished and boxed up before the Thompsons come to pick it up this afternoon. We have a bakery to run, which means there's no time for dilly-dallying."

I pulled my shoulders back, wondering if my mother was pleased with my take-charge attitude with running my own shop.

Zach turned to the side and coughed to hide the laughter that was coming out of him.

"Yes, ma'am," he replied, turning his back to my parents.

"Andi!" my mom hissed. "I thought you were going to introduce us to your new boyfriend," she said through tightly gritted teeth, nodding very pointedly to Zach.

Oh shit. *That* was what she was hinting at.

"Oh. Yes. Right," I said, my eyes widening as I awkwardly approached Zach and wrapped my arm around his waist, even though his back was still to them. I looked up and found him grinning so hard that his cheeks had to have been hurting him.

"Mom, Dad, this is my boyfriend, Zach."

Zach lifted his hand and pinched the bridge of his nose as my parents stood there, an uncomfortable silence stretching between us.

Then, to save the day—again, Zach turned around, wrapped his arm around my waist, and pulled me closer to him.

"It's a pleasure to meet you both," he said, his smile already winning my mother over as her features softened.

"Well, since Andi doesn't seem to know her manners this morning, I'll go ahead and introduce myself," my mother scolded. "My name is Jenny, but everyone calls me Jen. This is my husband, Ross."

"Sorry, my brain is mush this week with all of the extra orders that have come in for holiday parties this weekend," I explained, not minding the way Zach's fingers feathered lightly over my skin as he brushed them up and down my arm, leaving a trail of goosebumps along the way.

"Speaking of," my mom started. "I've told the Hendricks that you'll be joining us tomorrow night for their annual Christmas Extravaganza. You haven't been to it in years. It would be nice for you to show up with us."

"I can't make it, Mom. I already told you that I have a holiday party to attend with Zach's family."

"And there's no way that you can do both? Even if you could stop by for just a few minutes. I know it would mean the world to them."

"I—"

"I forgot to tell you, baby. My parents had to move their party to next weekend," Zach said, grinning as I shot daggers at him with my eyes.

Did he *not* understand the assignment and that I didn't want to go?

"Oh!" My mother exclaimed, clapping her hands excitedly. "Well, there you go. Now it looks like you can attend both!"

I looked up at Zach and pierced him with a look.

"Well, we better get going. We still need to check into the hotel before we go shopping for a gift for the white elephant tomorrow night. Don't forget you will need to bring one too. All adults are required to play; that means you too, Zach." My mom pointed a perfectly polished finger at him.

"I umm…" I tried to get the words out, to find a way to get out of going to this stuffy party when Zach spoke first.

"It'll be my honor to join you guys at the party. Thank you for including me. I'll make sure Andi and I find the perfect gifts to take."

"Sounds great. We'll see you tomorrow. Andi has the address and I'll send her the invite so you guys have the information about the dress code and theme for this year." My mom wiggled her fingers as she waved goodbye and followed my dad out to the shop.

I spun around, my body alarmingly close to Zach's, and glared at him.

"What the hell was that?"

Two
Zach

I tried to take Andi seriously as she stood there, scowling at me. Her dark eyes were the most beautiful shade of chocolate and paired perfectly with her dark red hair, reminding me of chocolate-covered cherries.

"Seriously, what was that?" she demanded, hand planted firmly on her cute little waist.

"I was pretending to be your boyfriend." I shrugged.

"I get that, and I'm thankful for you going along with it, but the point of having a pretend boyfriend was to get me *out* of going to that party. Instead, you roped both of us into going!" She threw her hands up, her ponytail bouncing from the movement.

I had to refrain from entertaining thoughts of pulling said ponytail in the throes of passion after kissing Andi. I knew we were supposed to be pretending for the sake of her parents thinking that she had a new boyfriend, but fuck if that hadn't felt real.

"Do you honestly think your parents would buy your story that easily? Even if you got out of going to the party with them, what makes you think they wouldn't find another way to set you up with this guy? Maybe a dinner out and he's the surprise guest of honor?"

"Why would they do that?" she questioned, brows furrowed.

"I don't know; maybe they wouldn't." I shrugged. "But it seems to me that if they were pushing that hard to get you to go to this party, then they likely weren't going to buy the whole boyfriend story you just made up. Especially since it seems like you hadn't told them you were seeing anyone *until* now."

She scrunched her nose as she listened, and I had to look away so I didn't stare at her plump lips that begged to be kissed again.

"Going to the party and taking me with you tells them we're the real deal. If you want them to believe you have a boyfriend, you have to be willing to show them. Which means we'll be spending a whole lot of time together while they're here."

"Ugh," she sighed heavily, leaning back against the counter. "You're right."

"Gee, thanks," I teased. "If my memory serves me correctly, *you're* the one who came running in here, begging *me* to kiss *you* and asking me to pretend to be your boyfriend."

"Nope, you're right. I just didn't think any of it through before I put my foot in my mouth and created a lie that could bite me in the ass."

"Well then, don't let it."

I stepped closer to her, invading her space. Her eyes widened as she gripped the counter behind her tightly.

"How am I going to stop it?"

"Easy. You don't *pretend* to be dating me. You date me for real."

Her jaw fell open as she stared at me.

"You're kidding, right?"

"Nope. This was all your idea. I'm just going with it."

"I didn't say it was a *good* idea," she whispered quietly as my chest brushed against hers.

"Are you saying you don't think I'm worthy of being your boyfriend?" I asked, tipping her chin up with my finger. I had been attracted to Andi since the day I first stepped foot in Sugarplum Sweets. I'd come in for a pastry and left with a job—not that I regretted either.

"I didn't say that at all."

"Okay, then, what's the problem?"

"Well, we work together for one," she scoffed, trying to regulate her breathing as it came out shaky. "I'm your boss—isn't that *forbidden* or something?"

"I don't know." I grinned, loving the way her body felt so close to mine. "Is it in the employee handbook?"

"I have no idea," she muttered, closing her eyes.

"Well, since you *are* the boss, I'm sure you could make an amendment to the handbook if needed. What else?"

"I just don't know how we're going to manage doing this— how are we going to keep up with this façade long enough for my parents to believe it's true before they go back to

Witchita?"

"How long are they here for?"

"They leave right after New Years."

"Then I guess we have work to do."

"What does that mean?" she asked, clearly flustered by my words as I stepped away and headed back to the cake I was finishing.

"It means we have work to do." I winked at her over my shoulder as she stood there in a daze. "Orders are piling up, Andi. Gotta get moving."

"Right. Orders. I'm on it." She shook her head and pushed past me to grab the next few tickets. I knew that she was nervous about this whole fake dating thing, but that only made me want to spend more time with her. I had always found Andi attractive but would never act on it because she was my boss, yet I couldn't help but wonder if there wasn't some sort of Christmas miracle at play here, guiding us together after all.

Three
Andi

By the time we closed tonight, I was tired, and my feet were swollen and achy. Everyone else had left for the day, and Becky let me know she was locking up behind her since I would be in my office and wouldn't hear if anyone came in. I leaned back in my chair and kicked my feet up on the desk, thinking about how amazing a long, hot soak in a tub would feel. Too bad I didn't have one in my apartment.

I lived in a studio apartment, which suited me since I didn't need much space, and it kept the rent costs down, allowing me to have more funds available for Sugarplum Sweets if needed. Venturing out to start my own business had been intimidating, but once I stepped foot in Sugarplum Falls, I knew this was where I wanted to be. And what better way to thrive in a town obsessed with Christmas than to open a bakery that served the most delectable treats.

"You leaving soon?" Zach asked, startling me as he leaned against the doorframe.

"Shit!" I shouted, startled at my desk. I yanked my feet down and tried to steady myself as my chair went sliding across the hardwood floor beneath me. Zach rushed over and caught the back of it before I tipped over.

"You scared the shit out of me," I laughed, my heart hammering in my chest. "I thought you left with the others."

"No, I stuck around to line up the orders for tomorrow. I separated and prioritized them based on when they were being picked up and how long it would take to make each item. Everything is ready to go for the morning crew tomorrow."

He was still gripping my chair when I looked up at him.

"You did all of that?"

He nodded, slowly releasing his hands.

"Why?" I asked, turning toward him. "Don't get me wrong, I'm very grateful for it, but that's not your job. You didn't have to do that."

"I know." He shrugged. "I just wanted to help. It was a busy day, and it's already late. I didn't want you to be stuck here longer while you did it yourself."

I shook my head in disbelief.

"Thank you, Zach. That was very kind of you."

"Well, what kind of boyfriend would I be if I didn't help out where I could?" he asked playfully.

"I don't know, but I gotta admit that the *fake* boyfriend is already shaping up to treat me better than a lot of the *real* boyfriends I've had."

He pressed his lips into a thin line but didn't say anything.

"So, tell me about the party tomorrow. What do I need to know going in?"

He sat one butt cheek on the edge of my desk and waited for me to answer while all I could think about was Zach's ass being on my desk. I never would have thought about it before, much less obsessed over it, but after that kiss earlier, I saw him differently.

"Well," I started, clearing my throat. "The Hendricks are an eclectic couple. They are some of the nicest, most down-to-earth people I've ever met, but they also throw the craziest parties. Hence, why I'm so reluctant to go to this one."

"Come on, it can't be that bad," he laughed.

"Oh, trust me. It can."

I shifted in my chair and crossed my leg over my knee, struggling to get comfortable with my achy body.

"Last year, the theme for the party was gingerbread. Everyone had to dress up as a gingerbread man or woman, and they set up this maze of gingerbread houses in their backyard. It took them weeks to build them, and they even hired a local contractor to come in and help. They had well over twenty guys out there daily, building professional-grade gingerbread houses for the party. The food was gingerbread themed, and they even served gingerbread martinis."

"Wow, that is intense. I'm surprised I hadn't heard about it. Seems like the kind of thing you'd hear about in Sugarplum Falls."

"It totally is, but they live in Chesapeake Peak. Another reason I didn't want to go," I teased.

"How long of a drive is it?"

"About an hour, depending on the roads and traffic."

"Okay. I'll drive," he offered.

"You don't have to do that."

"How would it look if I let my *girlfriend* drive us to the party? That wouldn't be very gentleman-like at all, Andi. I'll drive, and you can take part in the festivities. Speaking of which, what's the theme this year?"

"Fa-la-la-la- Hol-ly-wood."

Zach pinched his brows together in confusion.

"Okay, I'm going to need more info."

"According to the information my mom sent me in the invite, it's a take on famous holiday movies. We have to dress up as a character from one, and then the person/couple with the best costume wins."

"What do we win?"

"I don't know. The prizes are always as crazy as the themes but tied in so it's all cohesive. Last year, someone won a giant gingerbread house—not as big as the ones they used for the maze, but still big enough to require several people to load it into a van to have it transported."

"Wow. That's intense."

"I know. See, this is why I don't want to go. There's too much pressure around it."

"I hope this year's prize is something awesome," Zach said, the excitement in his voice ignoring my concerns.

"Are you sure you want to do this?" I questioned.

"Yeah, why not? It could be fun to get dressed up and pretend to be someone else for the night."

"You mean like a *boyfriend*?" I teased.

"Exactly." He winked. "Why aren't you more excited about this?"

"Because this is the equivalent of the childhood nightmare I had of going to school with no clothes on and everyone laughing at me."

"I can't think of any holiday movies that contain a lot of nudity, but we could try to make it happen." His grin was back on his adorable face, making his blue eyes glimmer.

"You know what I mean." I leaned forward and shoved his leg playfully.

His hand caught mine and held it for a brief second, forcing my breath to catch in my throat.

"If we're going to convince people that we're in a relationship, you can't freeze up every time I touch you," he whispered, looking up and locking eyes with me.

I let out a shuddered breath as a chill ran through me.

"I'll try harder," I laughed. "I haven't had anyone touch me like that in so long, my body doesn't know what to do when it happens."

I immediately froze as I realized the words that had just come out of my mouth. Shit!

"I mean… Um."

"You're fine, Andi." He hopped down from the desk and let go of my hand. "So, do you want to go shopping tomorrow morning for the party? Then we can grab lunch before we start getting ready and go over the details of our relationship. That way, neither of us are caught off guard."

"Sure. Sounds great."

I glanced at the clock on my computer and tried to stifle the groan about how late it was.

"You ready to head out?" he asked, noticing the distraction.

"Yeah. You?"

That was a stupid thing to ask, given that I was the boss and the only one left who had a key to the building tonight. I pressed a hand to my head and closed my eyes.

"Yup. I'll walk you out." He chuckled under his breath, but I could still hear it.

I nodded, not bothering to say anything since I couldn't manage to keep from sounding like an idiot right now.

Once I had my stuff, I made sure everything was turned off before locking up and walking with Zach to our vehicles. His truck looked massive compared to my sedan, but somehow it fit him and his rugged good looks.

"What time should I pick you up tomorrow?" he asked, standing by my door as I opened it and set my purse inside.

"Oh, you don't have to do that. I can meet you somewhere."

"Don't you think it might be kind of odd if I don't know where my girlfriend lives?"

I pulled my mouth to the side. I hadn't thought about that. Hell, I hadn't thought about a lot of the small details that went into having a fake relationship.

"Right," I said softly. "I'll text you my address. You can

pick me up at 9 if that works for you?"

"Sounds great. I'll see you in the morning."

I grinned, not knowing whether I should reach out and hug him. We were only fake dating, so it shouldn't mean that we had to pretend when no one was around to see us, but that still left me feeling unsure about the whole thing.

He fought back another chuckle while he held my door open as I climbed inside and then shut it. I waited until he was in his truck before pulling out and heading home to question every single decision I made today.

Four
Zach

I showed up at 9 a.m. on the dot, two peppermint mocha lattes in hand as I knocked on Andi's door and waited. A few minutes later, she opened the door, looking slightly frazzled until I extended her cup to her.

"You're a saint," she sighed, accepting it and lifting it to her lips. "Thank you for this. How did you know my order?"

"Sam told me," I admitted. Everyone in town knew Sam because he had the best coffee shop in Sugarplum Falls, and Sam prided himself on knowing everyone's order in town.

"He's the best." She closed her door and locked it, not offering to take me inside for a tour, which was fine. I didn't want to push her too hard too fast, but eventually, I would have to at least ask what her apartment looked like before I found myself in a bind by saying something that wasn't true.

"Where did you want to go first?" Andi asked as she hopped up into the truck. She looked adorable in the oversized hoodie and joggers she was wearing, and I found myself wondering if I preferred it over the jeans and tight-fitting t-shirts she wore to work.

"Have you decided on a movie yet?" I asked, testing the waters.

"No. You?" She turned and studied me as she took another sip of her latte.

"I have an idea if you trust me."

"Why do I feel nervous already?"

"I think you're going to feel that way today, regardless. But I have a fun idea if you're willing to go with it."

"Okay," she said with a nervous laugh. "I'll trust you."

Twenty minutes later, I pulled up in front of a thrift shop just on the outskirts of Sugarplum Falls.

"Do you know what you're looking for?" she asked as we got out and headed inside.

"Yup."

"Are you going to tell me?"

"Nope."

"Really?" She laughed, gently nudging me in the side with her elbow.

I held the door open for her to walk inside, then pulled out my phone to the picture I had saved last night.

"You're kidding," she snorted, covering her mouth.

"I don't kid when it comes to Nakatomi Plaza. Yippee-ki-yay—"

"Okay, okay," she laughed, holding her hands up. "I get it. You're a Die Hard fan. But does it really count as a holiday movie?" She scrunched her nose up.

I pulled my head back in disbelief as an older man who worked there walked by.

"You two finding everything alright?" he asked, pushing his

bifocals back up the bridge of his nose.

"No. No sir, we're not."

Andi widened her eyes at me, threatening me not to do it.

"Alright, son, what can I help you with."

"She just told me that Die Hard *doesn't* count as a holiday movie. Can you believe that?"

He looked from me to her, then back to me.

"No. I can't believe that. Die Hard is one of the best holiday movies there is. It's not Christmas until John McClane saves Holly at Nakatomi Plaza."

"Exactly. Do you think this disagreement is grounds for a breakup?" I asked, whispering loudly behind my hand so Andi could hear. She rolled her eyes as she struggled not to smile.

"A breakup might be a bit harsh, but I would definitely keep an eye on her. Next thing you know, she'll be saying that pineapple belongs on pizza."

I could see Andi open her mouth to confirm it did, but then she snapped it shut and looked away. I could see the humor dancing in her eyes, and it did something to me. It wasn't that I wasn't used to seeing her laugh and be happy, but I was now seeing it in a different light.

"So, what do you say, Andi? Are we on board with Die Hard for our costumes?" I asked, patting the older gentleman on the back as he walked past and went to put away some kid toys while mumbling about how Die Hard is a true classic and young kids just don't understand.

"Sure. I trust you. Who am I supposed to be?"

"Have you ever seen Die Hard?" I asked as I led her through the men's clothing and found what I was looking for. I grabbed a white wife beater and a pair of black pants and hung them over my arm.

"Nope."

"Seriously?"

"I guess it just never came up as something my family watched. We spent our holidays watching movies about Santa Claus and reindeer. Not action movies with people getting killed."

I glanced down at my watch.

"It's still early. We should have plenty of time to watch it before we go tonight."

"You're kidding, right?"

"Nope. Again, I don't kid when it comes to Die Hard."

She laughed and followed me to the women's section to pick out pieces that would fit what she needed. An hour later, we had everything we needed after stopping at a few other stores. I helped Andi carry her bags inside and worked on finding a copy of Die Hard to watch while she unpacked everything and wrapped the white elephant gifts.

"Are you ready for the best movie of your life?" I asked as she joined me on the couch.

"Bring it on," she giggled, curling into the couch and cuddling a pillow against her stomach. I turned my attention to the TV so I could avoid staring at how cute she looked.

Five
Andi

"I can't believe I let you talk me into this," I murmured as we pulled into the packed wraparound driveway, and Zach found a spot to park.

"What? You look great. We totally pulled this off." He turned off the engine and then looked at me.

"Not this," I said, moving my hands down my body. "I mean the party. I can't believe I let you talk me into going."

"Yeah, well, I figured your parents would have a hard time believing we both caught leptospirosis since we last saw them."

"You never know." I shrugged.

"Well, I haven't been around feral swine recently, have you?" He arched an eyebrow at me.

"That's debatable," I said, the corners of my lips turning up as I remembered the last store we had gone to and the unruly, grumpy old man who didn't want to help us even though he was the only one there.

"I won't assume that was about me," he teased with playfully narrowed eyes. "But I do want to get a picture of us before we go in, if that's okay."

"Sure."

I unbuckled and leaned closer as he pulled his cell phone out and flipped the camera for a selfie. He turned the light on since it was dark in the truck, and we both held our smiles while we waited for it to take.

"We should take a few more," I suggested, clearly stalling. "You know, just to make sure you got at least one good one since we went through all the effort to look this good."

We smiled, and I tried to ignore the butterflies swarming in my stomach from how close we were. He took a few pictures, checked them, then smiled and put his phone back in his pocket.

"Alright. We can't hide in here forever. John McClane certainly didn't. So what do you say, Andi? Are you ready for this?" He reached up and turned the light off.

"Since there's no turning back, I guess we should get going."

I smiled and reached for the door, only for Zach to rush around and open it for me. His hair was disheveled, his shirt smeared with red paint to look like blood, and a cigarette hung out of the side of his mouth. There was no question about who he was supposed to be.

I climbed out and smoothed down my long black skirt, making sure the belt was still in place. It was hard to believe that we were able to find a pinkish-colored velour button-down shirt so easily, but it pulled the final look together. A few hours ago, I had no idea who Holly Gennaro McClane was, but now I felt like her twin with my hair-spray-saturated hairdo and outfit.

We walked to the door and rang the doorbell, my nerves getting the better of me.

"No freaking way," Mr. Hendricks said, tipping his head back with laughter. "Frannie, you gotta come see this!"

His wife came rushing through the crowd, pushing her small glasses up her nose as she struggled to move in the heavy Mrs. Claus dress she had on that matched his Santa outfit.

"Oh my goodness!" She grinned and held her hands to her rosy cheeks. "You two look amazing!"

"Welcome to the party," Mr. Hendricks said, winking to make sure we caught the line from the movie.

"Yippee-Ki-Yay, Motherf—"

"That's enough," I playfully scolded, shaking my head as if he was truly a bother. I nudged him in the ribs with my elbow, earning his hand slipping around my waist as he pulled me close. "I can't take him anywhere without him causing a scene."

"It seems you've brought a rowdy one," Mr. Hendricks teased. "Guess he's going to keep us all in our place."

"Or drive you crazy," Zach joked with a wink as he stepped inside and guided me with his hand firmly placed on my lower back.

"Well, I am Santa," Mr. Hendricks said, deepening his voice and rubbing his padded stomach. "I've got my list and can see right here that you're on the nice list." He produced a rolled-up piece of paper from his pocket.

"I don't know about that, Santa."

"Trust me; it takes a lot for me to move someone to the naughty list."

"I give it five minutes, and then you'll change your mind. I mean, only John can drive somebody that crazy," I laughed, impressed that I had memorized the line Zach had given me.

Everyone laughed as we moved inside the house, my nerves finally calming.

Mr. and Mrs. Hendricks excused themselves to tend to the kitchen while Zach and I walked around, looking for my parents. I knew a handful of people from previous parties, but not enough that I wanted to go over and say hi.

Zach stayed by my side, hand possessively on my lower back as we moved from the living room to the dining room, where there were tables of food set out.

I walked slowly, looking at all the options while Zach handed me a plate. I looked up and smiled, thankful he wasn't feeling out of sorts here. If anything, *he* was the calm one who seemed like he belonged here, and I was the nervous wreck.

The food was adorable, completely tying in the Hollywood theme with glimmer and glam. My eyes roamed over the options, my smile widening when I saw the Black Tie Brie bites with the black olives cut into small pieces to look like a tie. I added a few Walk of Fame star sugar cookies to my plate before offering Zach some, then moved to the next table.

We both indulged in the Hollywood Star cheese board, pairing them with sliced meats and crackers. I wasn't sure how I was going to eat all of this food, but then my stomach grumbled loudly, and Zach chuckled as he added a star-studded popcorn ball to my plate.

Once we were done filling our plates, we grabbed a seat

in the corner at one of the bistro tables set up in the living room. It wasn't unusual for the Hendricks to have all their furniture moved out of the giant space and stored in another room for the parties so more seating arrangements could be brought in. One year, the theme revolved around sock hops, and they had the cutest booths brought in and turned the living room into a diner.

It was loud around us as everyone mingled and talked, but we were hungry and kept our attention on the food until a waiter passed by and offered confetti champagne that we couldn't resist.

We were so deeply engrossed in our feast that we didn't hear my parents until they sat beside us.

"Well, aren't you two just the cutest? I'm surprised Andi agreed to go as Holly since she hasn't seen the movie before," my mom said, offering a sweet smile.

"We watched it earlier," I replied, covering my mouth with a napkin because I refused to stop eating long enough to talk.

"Is that so?" My mom's grin spread wider as she looked between us.

"It is," Zach answered, wiping his mouth with the napkin before tossing it to his empty plate. "We went shopping this morning and then hung out at her place, watching the movie to make sure we got all of the details correct."

"It looks like you succeeded," my dad offered, adjusting the antlers on his head.

"You guys, too. Rudolf and Clarice, very cute!" I said, finally finishing my food.

"Yeah, but we're not the *only* ones," my mom said, irritation thick in her voice as she adjusted her fake eyelashes. "It's going to be hard to stand out when there are at least a dozen others."

I giggled at how seriously she was taking this and then looked away when she pinned me with a look. Zach and Dad talked for a while, bullshitting about the weather and whatnot, while my mom eyed her competition.

<u>Six</u>
Zach

The party seemed to be going smoothly, so I wasn't sure what Andi was so stressed about. By the third glass of glitter champagne, she didn't look like she had a care in the world as she clung to my side and flirted shamelessly with me.

I wasn't sure if it was just an act or if there was something more there that she was letting through now that she felt less inhibited. I knew that I had felt the chemistry between us when we kissed, but I wasn't going to trust her judgment right now when she was clearly tipsy.

People continued to come by and compliment us on our outfits, and surprisingly enough, we were the only ones to do Die Hard. There were also plenty of arguments about whether it was a holiday movie or not, but Mr. Hendricks shut it down quickly by putting it on the giant projector screen in the backyard, where the rest of the party was happening.

The night felt like it was flying by, and when Andi started yawning, I wondered if I should call it a night and get her home.

"Alright, everyone," Mrs. Hendricks yelled loudly, gaining everyone's attention. "It's that time! Get your numbers out for the white elephant game!"

We all piled into the living room and sat in a circle after the hired helpers arranged the chairs so we could all face each other.

"Who has number one?" Mr. Hendricks asked, looking around the room.

A very pregnant woman dressed as the Grinch got up and handed her ticket in before selecting a gift from the table. She shook it gently, set it down, and grabbed a larger box from the back. Everyone made noises as they either encouraged her to take it or put it back, depending on what they wanted. The gifts were set at a maximum of $50 and were intended to be gag gifts.

She smiled and put the box back before grabbing a smaller one and opening it.

Inside was a snowman coffee mug with a string of marshmallows attached to the back, making it look like it was leaving a trail of poop.

The next few people went and I anxiously waited until Andi's turn since she had drawn ticket number eight. The other gifts were funny, but nothing anyone wanted to trade for. A blanket that looked like a slice of cheese, a pair of bunny slippers with ears that extended to the side and slapped the floor as you walked, and a bottle of homemade liquid courage, but no one knew what was inside.

Finally, it was Andi's turn. Her cheeks flushed the cutest shade of pink as she got up and scanned the table. She looked at me, asking what I thought, but I just shrugged. I had no idea what to vote for and there wasn't anything that she was impressed with so far.

She went for the biggest box on the table, her grin spreading across her face as she unwrapped a 6' inflatable elf lawn decoration. Everyone clapped as she returned to her seat and showed me.

"It's so cute!" she squealed. "I can't put it up at my apartment, but it would be so cute at the shop!"

"It will look great there. I can help you set it up this week if you'd like."

"That would be wonderful. Thank you."

We locked eyes and almost forgot where we were when she leaned in close, our lips almost brushing against each other.

"Alright, number twelve, you're up!" Mr. Hendricks announced.

We watched Andi's dad select a gift from the table, looking less than thrilled about the salt and pepper shakers in his hand. One was Santa, the other Mrs. Claus, but instead of being the cute couple everyone thought they were, they were bent over with their butts as the top of the shakers. He shook his head, keeping the grin at bay as he sat beside Andi's mom.

The game continued with people getting to the point that they started stealing gifts that had already been open, aside from the one Andi was clutching to her chest. I didn't expect anyone to ask for it with the way she would snarl whenever anyone glanced at her. It was the same expression I had seen earlier when she pointed out the guy her parents wanted to set her up with. Thankfully, he had found a single woman in the crowd who didn't mind his company and didn't bother us.

The last few gifts remained on the table and I looked around, wondering who still had to go. I knew I had the last number, but I couldn't spot anyone without a gift in their hand already, yet there were two extra gifts on the table.

"It's the final number," Mrs. Hendricks announced happily, looking directly at me. "Let's see if this gift meets Mr.

McClane's standards." She extended her hand to the table, inviting me to go up and pick a gift.

"But there's more than one left," I said quietly as she joined me.

"The other two are for me and Mr. Hendricks. We don't like to go until everyone else has."

"I see." I smiled and picked up the small box on the table, noticing a giggle from the pregnant woman as she wiggled in her seat.

"Pick that one," she said happily, looking from me to Andi. "Trust me, it won't disappoint."

I eyed her suspiciously as I unwrapped it, finding a black box with the words Dark Vibes printed on the outside.

I opened it and paused for a moment, looking from it to the woman.

"Is this what I think it is?" I asked.

She nodded, steepling her fingers together in front of her.

"What is it?" someone called from the circle.

I turned to Andi and lifted it, showing everyone.

"A candy cane shaped vibrator."

<u>Seven</u>
Andi

The party had gone better than expected, probably because I was there with Zach and not some random guy my parents were trying to set me up with. After the white elephant exchange, we said our goodbyes and headed out with the candy cane vibrator and a giant inflatable elf. We also won the costume contest and took home a gift certificate to an upscale steakhouse in Sugarplum Falls, as well as a spa package with a ninety-minute couples massage. Not a bad night, if I do say so myself.

We talked the entire drive back to my apartment, and I found it odd how easy it was to be around Zach. Sure, we worked well together at the shop, but it was different when we weren't in a boss-employee environment. Zach was fun at work, but Zach outside of work was someone I found myself wanting to get to know better.

"Did you have fun tonight?" Zach asked as he waited to take the turn to my street. The snow was lightly falling, making the night look peaceful despite a bad storm on the way.

"I did. Thank you for going with me."

"Thank you for inviting me."

"Well, technically, I didn't. My mom did. I was trying to get us *out* of going. Remember?"

"Yeah, but you wouldn't have won Elfie if you didn't go."

"You named my elf?" I asked, laughing.

"I did. I like to name things."

"So, does that mean you named your prize as well?" I questioned, pulling my lip between my teeth.

"Heck yeah, I did."

"Oh my God, I gotta hear this." I tipped my head back and laughed before turning to face him. "What exactly did you name your vibrator?"

"Candy," he said matter of factly before taking the turn.

"Candy?" I pinched my brows together to try to figure out why he chose that, but the champagne still made my head feel fuzzy. "Why Candy?"

"Well, it's a candy cane, for one. Two, no one will think about it if I ask you if you want to hang out with Candy tonight."

Heat flushed through my body.

"Why would you ask *me* that?" I whispered, struggling to find my voice.

"Why wouldn't I? You are my girlfriend, after all. It might be a little inappropriate if I asked someone else."

He pulled into the parking lot of my apartment complex and found a spot close to mine.

"Oh, good point," I said nervously, shaking my head. "Well, thanks for going with me tonight. Have fun with Candy. Or not. Whatever, I don't need to know." I shook my head.

I rambled when I was nervous, which was never flattering. I pulled the handle to open the door and found Zach on the other side, waiting for me.

He extended his hand and helped me down before taking the giant box from me.

"Do you want to leave this in my truck?" he offered. "That way you don't have to take it up to your apartment and then bring it back down just to take it to work."

"Are you sure you don't mind?"

"Not at all. I'll get it up for you later this week."

My eyes widened as my head tilted to the side.

"The inflatable elf, Andi. I'll get the inflatable elf up for you later this week."

"Oh. Yeah. Duh." I sucked in a deep breath and forced myself to let it out slowly.

We walked quickly to my apartment, trying to escape the bitter cold as the wind whipped snow flurries in our faces. Once we got to the door, I hurried to unlock it and waited for him to come in before bothering to ask if he wanted to.

"Sorry, I shouldn't have assumed you wanted to come in," I said, still holding the door open as I looked down in embarrassment.

"Don't be." He shut the door for me, then his hands found my hips and pushed me back against the door before he leaned in and kissed me.

I moaned softly as his tongue teased mine, the warmth of his mouth welcoming as he deepened the kiss. Our hands roamed each other's bodies, his exploring my ribs and gently grazing my breasts while mine worked on getting his leather jacket off him.

Suddenly, the realization of what we were doing rushed over me. I dropped my hands to my sides, leaving his jacket hanging oddly down his body.

My cheeks flushed with embarrassment as I looked away, ashamed for leading him on the way I had.

 He nodded as he rubbed a finger across his lips as if this explained everything.

"I'm sorry," he said, stepping back and shoving his hands in his pockets once his jacket was situated again.

"No, it's my fault. I'm sorry."

"I should get going."

I nodded subtly, still refusing to meet his eyes.

"Andi?"

"Yeah?"

"It would really help if you look at me when I tell you what I'm about to."

My eyes lifted slowly, only to find him watching me.

"I know it's hard for you to allow yourself to cross this line with me but trust me—I will never do anything that makes you uncomfortable. Whether this is a fake relationship or not doesn't matter. I respect you, Andi."

"Thank you." I swallowed hard, trying to force the emotions down.

"I'll see you on Monday. Thank you for a fun night, Andi."

"Thank you for coming with me. Believe it or not, I had fun too."

He winked and pulled open the door, bringing in a gust of wind with him.

I lifted my hand to shield my face.

"Are you sure you want to go out in this?" I asked, my voice muffled behind my arm.

"Yeah, I'll be fine. Good night."

He pulled the door closed behind him and I hated the nagging feeling that said I should have invited him to stay.

I curled up on the couch with a blanket and turned on the TV, unsure what to watch until I saw the next Die-Hard movie pop up on the streaming app. I clicked it and got ready to watch John McClane save the day.

Eight
Zach

Monday morning came around before I was ready, and we were slammed with holiday orders the moment Sugarplum Sweets opened the doors.

"I know that it's a lot to ask, but we're really in a bind," Jasmin said, holding her hands together as she begged.

"Have you checked with Carmen? I know she's been doing some side orders." I checked the planner again, hoping I had missed something. Carmen was the sweetest woman and recently decided to dip her toes in the catering business, so it was a possibility that she might be able to help Jasmin.

"I did. She just took on a holiday party for Mason, Inc. It's bigger than what she's done before, so she's not taking anything else right now."

I scrubbed a hand down my face and studied her. I didn't want to say no to her, but when I stared at the schedule that was already filled with custom orders, I knew there was no way we could pull this off. It was less than two weeks until Christmas, and we were swamped.

"I'll have to ask Andi and see if—"

"See what?" she asked, startling me as she came around the corner and joined us at the counter.

I grinned at the sight of her, loving the way her red hair caught in the lights above us in the cute ponytail she had it in.

"Jasmin needs a custom order for 12 dozen sugar cookies for the Frosty Fest parade this weekend," I said softly, giving both of them a warm smile.

Andi's eyes widened as she took the number in, then leaned forward and checked the schedule.

"I've checked to see if we can fit it in, but we're booked solid through Saturday."

She nodded, exhaling slowly while her finger trailed across the days, looking for any openings I might have missed.

"I'm really sorry to ask," Jasmin said. "If I would have known that my usual baker was going to get the flu, I would have planned this *weeks* in advance with you."

Andi arched an eyebrow and glanced up.

"You're cheating on me with another baker?" she teased playfully, returning her attention to the planner.

"You know you're still my number one girl," Jasmin laughed. "But Glenda has been making the cookies for the parade since I was a little girl. It's just tradition. Or it was until this year."

Andi sighed heavily and lifted her head, her features softening once she took in the stress etched on Jasmin's face.

"I wouldn't normally do this, *but* since you're in a bind and no one wants to screw up the Frosty Fest, I'll make them for you."

My eyes bulged out of my head.

"We don't have the staff to do this, Andi," I whispered,

trying not to draw anyone's attention or embarrass either of them.

"I know." She pulled her shoulders back, and I watched the determination on her face. "I will do them after hours. I'll stay late Wednesday, Thursday, and Friday and get them done; that way, they'll be fresh for Saturday."

"Oh, gosh, no! I can't ask you to do that," Jasmin said, shaking her head.

Andi placed a hand on her hip and pinned Jasmin with a look that got her to stop arguing.

"I'll have the cookies ready by Saturday morning. I can drop them off before everything starts since I'll have a booth there anyway. Do you need anything else?"

"No, thank you. I already have the candy canes for everyone on the floats to pass out. The only thing that I was missing was the cookies. The volunteers look forward to them every year, and I didn't have the heart to tell them we wouldn't have them this year."

"I get it," Andi said with a smile. "I'll call on Saturday when I'm heading over so someone can help unload."

"Okay. Thank you." Jasmin sighed heavily, a weight lifted from her shoulders.

Andi went over to the registers to help Becky with the line that was wrapping around the wall and out the door. Soon, the local moms would be coming in with their toddlers for the sugar cookie decorating class and Andi's attention would be pulled to that. Needless to say, she was a force to be reckoned with when it came to her business. She never sat on the sidelines as she was always involved in everything happening.

I rang Jasmin up for the custom order and took down the details of what she wanted. I knew she had a standard order she went with every year from her regular baker, but I could tell she was trying not to create too much work for Andi. Finally, she decided on a mixture of Santa, reindeer, and Christmas trees, which would keep it easy for Andi with the amount of decorating she had to do.

After she left, I leaned back for a second and watched Andi as she moved throughout the shop, smiling at people and acting as if she didn't have a care in the world. I was already stressed with the amount of work she had ahead of her with less than two weeks until Christmas, but Andi didn't seem to care. Or maybe that's just what she wanted people to think.

I spent the afternoon in the back, cranking through orders while everyone scrambled to stay caught up. We had an amazing team that allowed us to work without having to constantly check in with each other. I grabbed the next ticket from the rack and read it off, noting what I needed before I started.

The cakes that were being picked up today were already boxed up and set in the pick-up area for the staff up front to grab when the customers came in. I was already working on tomorrow's orders and hoped to get ahead if possible. I knew that in addition to the custom orders, we still needed to keep inventory stocked in the store, which meant that I needed to get going on replenishing the chocolate truffles that seemed to be selling like wildfire.

"Hey," Andi said, leaning next to me to see what I was working on. "Those look amazing."

"Thank you. I'm almost done with these and was getting

ready to start on the truffles. I was wondering if it's okay with you if I make some snowballs? They're white chocolate and coconut truffles."

"Sounds good to me. But don't forget to stop and take a break. You've been going all morning and I haven't had a chance to see who has taken a lunch and who still needs one."

"I'm good," I said with a smile, but the scowl on her face said she didn't believe me.

"Zach," she warned, hands planted on her hips again. "Please stop and take a break."

"I will when you do."

She arched an eyebrow and folded her arms over her chest as I turned and matched her stance.

"I thought *I* was the boss."

"Yeah, but *I'm* the boyfriend. And what kind of guy would I be if I wasn't concerned about taking care of my girlfriend?"

She shook her head and rolled her eyes.

"You're only my boyfriend when my parents are around, so that logic doesn't work here."

"Are you sure about that?" I asked, nodding to the window behind her that opened to the lobby where her parents stood in line, waving when they spotted us.

Nine
Andi

"Mom, Dad, what are you guys doing here?" I asked in surprise as my parents made their way back to the kitchen to greet me. Zach smirked and finished the last few truffles, then wiped his hand on his apron before shaking my dad's.

"We were in the area and decided we needed more of those delicious scones we had yesterday. Are you busy?" my mom asked, looking between Zach and me.

"I'm actually sw—"

"Andi was just getting ready to go grab some lunch. It's been super busy, and she was reminding me that we haven't taken a break since we got here." Zach extended his arm around my waist, pulling me into his side as I tried to ignore how fast my heart raced from his touch.

"Oh, wonderful!" Mom exclaimed, throwing her hands in the air. "We were going to grab lunch too. Why don't we go together?"

"I'm sorry, Mom. I really wish we could. Unfortunately, things are so busy right now that I only have a few minutes to grab a quick bite. Maybe another time?"

My mom scowled and studied me the way she always did when she suspected I was lying.

"I thought you were getting ready to go grab lunch?" she questioned, looking at Zach.

"We were," I said as steadily as I could. I hated lying, and the break in my voice always gave me away. "But we were just going to run to McDonald's and come straight back. And honestly, I don't see why *both* of us need to go, *darling*." My jaw hurt from how tight I was gritting the words out. "Won't you be a doll and pick something up for us while I keep things going here?"

I looked up at Zach and tried to give him my best lovey-dovey girlfriend look, but the humor dancing in his eyes called my bluff.

"Well, I would, however, I know how much you like to be in charge. You were just saying you wanted to get out for a few minutes." He leaned forward and whispered behind his hand so my parents could hear him. "I think she really wants to sneak out so she can kiss me, you know, since we haven't told anyone at work yet."

My mother's eyes widened as my face turned bright red. I could see the corners of my dad's lips turn up as he tried to hide his amusement.

"They don't know?" my mother asked in disbelief as she leaned closer.

"No." I shook my head, already seeing how much my mother loved this. She spent her days watching soap operas, and now she was getting a first-hand look at some real-life drama— even if we were just pretending.

"Don't worry. Your secret is safe with me." She pretended to zip her mouth shut and throw away the key.

"So, are we going to get lunch or not?" my father asked, shifting his weight.

"Zach, why don't you head out first, and then we'll leave a few minutes later with Andi." My mom winked, making herself completely obvious to anyone who might have been looking.

"Mom, really, I don't think—"

"Sure, that sounds great. I'll see you guys in a few minutes."

Zach leaned down and kissed my head quickly before taking off his apron and grabbing his stuff from the lockers in the back. He grinned on his way out, leaving me alone with my parents as I secretly plotted his death.

I was thankful that most of the staff was up front so no one had seen the exchange between me and Zach; however, I was starting to get nervous that someone would see something and start asking questions. Sugarplum Falls was a super small town, so joining Zach for lunch at McDonald's would be enough to get the gossip mill going.

I sent my parents to wait for me in their car while I took care of a few things in the shop. Liv was my assistant manager, so I told her where we were with things and asked her to have Becky take over where Zach had left off. Once I was confident that the store wouldn't burn down while I was gone, I grabbed my stuff and headed out.

I sat in the backseat of my parents' SUV, still stewing over getting stuck going to lunch with my parents when I texted Zach.

Me: What in the world were you thinking?

Zach: You do remember that we're supposed to be dating, right?

Me: Yes. But you can't keep volunteering for us to go places with my parents.

Zach: I might be wrong, but I'm pretty sure that was the whole point of me pretending to be your boyfriend. Unless you had ulterior motives I don't know about.

Me: Very funny.

Zach: You're avoiding the question…

I stuffed my phone back into my pocket as my dad parked, and we got out. It wasn't that I had ulterior motives when I first asked him to pretend to be my boyfriend, but after that kiss on Saturday, I was having a hard time pretending that I *hadn't* felt something.

Zach was already inside, waiting at the counter when we arrived.

I stood next to him as we waited in line, completely surprised when he knew my order when we got to the register. I knew I was predictable, given that I always ordered the same thing, but I had never gone to lunch with Zach before, so I was taken aback by how well he seemed to know me.

We sat at a table in the back, and my mom glanced around, scanning the tables before whispering in a not-so-hushed tone.

"Do you know any of these people?" she asked behind her hand.

"Yes, Mom. I know almost all of them."

"Are they going to tell everyone that you're dating?" she

questioned, her voice slightly lower after my father shot a look at her.

"No, they'll probably wonder why Zach came to lunch with us, but it won't be a big deal. People will get bored and talk about who still hasn't decorated for Christmas yet or compare who has the best lawn decorations."

"We could just make it official and announce it to everyone," Zach offered, his blue eyes finding mine as he looked up after taking a bite of his burger.

I grinned tightly as I tried to keep myself together. We were doing well, and I didn't want to blow our cover in front of my parents right now. There was enough going on without having to explain to them that I lied about having a boyfriend, let alone that Zach felt bad enough for me to go along with it.

"That's not necessary," I gritted, swinging my foot hard under the table to kick him.

"Ouch!" my mother gasped, reaching down to rub her leg. "Andi Rose! Why on earth did you just kick me?"

"I'm so sorry!" My eyes widened in horror as I covered my mouth. Zach turned his head to cough, and I couldn't tell if it was to keep from laughing or because he was about to choke on his bite that he didn't get to chew before it started down his throat.

It might not be so hard to kill him after all.

"Why did you do that?" she asked again, still rubbing it.

"It was an accident," I lied, feeling my whole face flame with embarrassment. "I've been getting these involuntary muscle spasms in my legs. The doctor thinks it's from being on my feet for so long at work."

"Well, you better get that looked at again," my dad said sternly before lifting his sandwich to his mouth.

"Yeah," I sighed heavily, leaning back in my chair, my appetite completely gone. "I'll be sure to do that."

Ten
Zach

"Can I get a large peppermint mocha latte with extra whipped cream and a large salted caramel cold brew?" I tapped my debit card against the steering wheel while Andi stared out the passenger window. I knew she was still irritated, though I wasn't sure if it was with me or her parents for pushing her to have lunch with them.

I pulled forward and paid for our drinks, knowing she needed the afternoon pick-me-up. I also knew that peppermint mocha lattes were Andi's weakness, and *if* I were on her bad side, this might be the way to redeem myself.

Sugarplum Lattes was close enough to walk to from Sugarplum Sweets; however, the snow coming down was enough to warrant using the drive-through on our way back from lunch.

Andi hadn't said much after the whole kicking incident, and I felt bad that I had pushed her so hard. But she knew as well as I did that we couldn't keep pretending to date for her parents without everyone in town finding out. Whether or not she thought about that when she proposed our little arrangement was beyond me.

I grabbed the drinks and set them in the cup holders between us before crossing the parking lot and finding a spot close enough to the shop without having to trek through a ton of snow. At the rate it was coming down, I wouldn't be surprised if other places didn't start closing soon. I already knew that Andi would stay open until the last order of the day was picked up because that was just how she was. She didn't like to fall through on her commitments, which meant that she would risk driving in terrible weather just to make sure everyone got their orders that day.

"Hey, before we go in," I started, turning to look at her as her hand hovered over the handle to get out. "I just wanted to say I'm sorry. I didn't mean to make you uncomfortable or to put you on the spot. But I think we're going to have to eventually tell people that we're dating if you want this to work for your parents."

"I know," she sighed softly, leaning back into the seat.

"Or we could always break up," I offered, though I hated the words the second they touched my tongue. "I mean, the party is over, so I don't think you have to worry about them trying to set you up anymore."

"I thought about that," she admitted.

"But?" I chewed the inside of my cheek as I waited for the words I *hoped* she would say.

But I realized that I don't want to pretend with you anymore.

"But we had dinner on Sunday, and they told me that seeing me this happy was the best gift they could have ever asked for." She looked at me, and I noticed the tears in her eyes. "If I tell them that we broke up, they're going to be devastated. I can't ruin Christmas by breaking their hearts."

"So, what you're saying is that we're stuck together for the foreseeable future?" I asked, my grin giving away how excited I was about this so-called problem.

"It would look that way," she said with a soft laugh. "But you were right."

My heart raced as I waited again for her to admit her true feelings for me.

"I was?"

"Yeah. We can't just pretend for my parents."

"Does that mean I get to officially be your boyfriend and tell everyone you're mine?"

She nodded and rolled her eyes.

"I can tell how excited you are," I teased sarcastically.

"I suck at lying, and this is A LOT of lying. It's hard for me to pretend to be something I'm not."

"So then don't."

She moved her purse strap back up her arm and looked at me.

"Don't what?"

"Don't pretend. Date me for real."

She rolled her eyes again and laughed as she reached for the handle to get out. I grabbed our drinks as she opened the door and got out. The gust of cold air was all it took to clear my head and remind me that while I wanted nothing more than for this to be real between us, she wasn't on the same page.

Once inside, I got back to work in the kitchen while Andi made her way through the front, checking on things and getting updates on what orders still needed to be picked up. She sent most of the staff home so they wouldn't have to worry about the roads getting worse by the time they left.

That left Andi manning the register while I did my thing in the kitchen.

Andi had tried to send me home, too, but there was no way in hell I was leaving her by herself to close up. I wanted to make sure that she got home okay, even if that meant I had to sneak around and follow her to her apartment. I felt overly protective of her, even though I wasn't *technically* her boyfriend.

A few hours passed, and I had a good head start on the items going out tomorrow. I also had plenty of pastries made for the morning, so Andi wouldn't have to do much when she opened, other than bake the ones she preferred to make fresh daily.

"Hey, how's it going back here?" she asked, popping her head in the window from up front.

"Not too bad. I've got the first orders for tomorrow boxed up and ready. How are things up there?"

"Good. Slow. We're just waiting for two more orders to be picked up. Then, we can call it a day and close early."

I nodded and wiped down the counter.

"You can go now if you want," she offered again.

"Nope. I'm not leaving until you do."

I stood behind the metal island and folded my arms over my chest.

"I'll be fine. Really. I'd feel better if you got out of here before the storm worsens."

"And I would feel better if you let me drive you home."

"Why would I do that?"

"So I know that you made it home safely."

"But then I wouldn't have a car and wouldn't be able to get here in the morning to open."

"I'll come pick you up." I shrugged as if it wasn't a big deal because it wasn't. I didn't mind driving Andi around, especially since her car didn't look well equipped to handle the regular storms we got to begin with. This one was like a blizzard on steroids.

"I can't have you going back and forth, dropping me off and picking me up." She laughed softly. "I appreciate the concern, but I'm fine. I promise."

I crossed the room and pushed through the door that separated us. I wasn't going to keep fighting with her through the small window. I needed her to hear me and listen when I said I wasn't backing off on this. We were now only inches apart, and I could see the way her chest rose and fell heavily as she reacted to the close proximity.

"Andi, I'm not going to fight you on this," I warned.

"Is that so?" She tilted her head and planted her hands on her hips.

God, I wanted to kiss her so badly. To wrap my lips over hers and eat the words she desperately wanted to say.

"It is."

"I don't think you have much say in it."

Her words were stern, but I heard the hitch in her voice, the same way it did when she lied to her parents.

I stepped closer, loving the way her body reacted to me. Her eyes dilated. Her lips moistened as her tongue ran across them. Her skin erupted in goosebumps along her arms.

"I'm telling you that one way or another, I'm making sure you get home safely, Andi. It's up to you whether you go voluntarily or if I have to throw you over my shoulder and carry you out caveman style, but you're going with me."

The bell chimed as a customer entered the store, forcing me to step back. I didn't bother to turn to see who it was. I locked eyes with Andi for a moment before I pushed through the door and returned to the kitchen.

I needed a moment to collect myself and tell my dick to stand down.

Eleven
Andi

"Thank you again for the coffee this afternoon," I said as I folded my hands in my lap and sat in the passenger seat of Zach's truck. While I wanted to stand my ground with him and prove that I didn't need him to take care of me, I realized I didn't stand a chance against the storm when my car was buried in a few feet of snow by the time we left. Though I would have put up more of a fight if we had time just to see the whole caveman thing come into play. But it was late, and I didn't want Zach to have any trouble getting home since he was already going out of his way to take me.

"You're welcome again." The dimples in his cheeks deepened with his grin. "Do you want to stop for dinner on the way home?"

I looked around us, not sure anything was still open. Not only that, I didn't want to tie up more of his time and delay him further.

"I'm okay, but thank you."

"What are you going to eat?" he asked with a cocked eyebrow.

"I don't know," I laughed. "But I'm sure I have something."

"The power went out at the shop when we left, Andi. It's likely going to be out at your house, too. Which means you're not going to be able to cook anything. Let me stop and grab something."

"I don't think anything is open," I replied, chewing my lip as I studied the options of fast-food places to see if anyone had a line. It was eerily dark and quiet. "Plus, I'm sure everyone is without power."

"It looks like Pizza Shack is up and running," he noted, pointing to the packed parking lot on the other side of the street.

The lights were on inside, which was promising. A lot of the businesses had started getting back up generators, but there were still a lot that didn't have them and would be closed until the storm passed and the power came back. Thankfully, I had invested in one before I opened. It had already saved my ass more times than I could count.

"Okay. Sounds good. Thank you."

He pulled into the parking lot and then parked.

"What kind of pizza do you like?"

"I'm not picky."

He tipped his head back and groaned.

"What?" I laughed, lifting my shoulders and then letting them fall.

"Can you please just tell me what you want?"

Well, that's a loaded question, isn't it?

"Okay, okay," I laughed. "I like the meat lover's."

In more ways than one. Maybe a Zach sausage…

"Alright. I'll be right back."

"You don't have to. I can g—" I started but stopped when he hopped out and slammed his door behind him.

I shook my head and took a calming, deep breath as I tried to remind myself that he was just being kind and that it didn't mean anything. I would give him cash for my food as soon as he got back into the truck, as well as some gas money.

It was surprisingly busy, yet the line seemed to move quickly. I assumed they had a constant supply of their Fast Fix pizzas, which were premade and kept in a warmer for people to grab in a hurry. Luckily, the meat lover's was one of them so hopefully Zach didn't have to wait long for one.

There was no way I could eat a whole pizza by myself, but it would come in handy for breakfast, lunch, and dinner for a few days if needed, especially if the power didn't come back soon.

I was making a list on my phone of things I needed to take care of tomorrow as soon as I got to the shop when Zach climbed in and handed me a stack of boxes as he sat a bag full of stuff in the back seat.

"What all did you get?" I laughed, noticing more than one pizza box on my lap.

"I decided to get the Margherita pizza as well. Then I realized that we needed breadsticks and dipping sauces. By the time I had all that, I found myself ordering a large chocolate dessert pizza."

"*We*?" I giggled, finding my mood lighter with his excitement over the food.

"Yeah, I thought we could have dinner together." He looked

at me out of the corner of his eye.

"Oh, okay." I wasn't sure what else to say.

Zach drove slowly even though no one else was on the road. But it didn't matter, since there was a solid block of ice beneath the blanket of snow we were driving on. Given how bad it had gotten, I was thankful I didn't have to drive in this after all. I knew the morning would be worse, but I didn't have the energy to worry about that right now as my stomach grumbled loudly from the heavenly aroma of the food.

We finally made it to my apartment, and Zach grabbed a spot by the sidewalk, which kept us from carrying all the food across the parking lot. There was already a mess of snow we would have to get through, but at least it wasn't as deep with the wind blowing it in the opposite direction.

I led the way, frowning when he insisted on carrying everything. I stepped carefully, trying to help navigate the path for us. Thankfully, his boots were made for this weather, whereas mine were more for cuteness than functionality. I'd have to plan better tomorrow and make sure that I was dressed appropriately.

I slid the key into the lock and pushed the door open, holding it for Zach before going in and locking it behind me. It was already getting cold in my apartment with the power being off, though at least it wasn't as frigid as it was outside.

"Sorry, it's going to be chilly in here," I apologized, rubbing my hands together as he set the food on the island. I was surprised he remembered where it was, given he had only been here once.

"No need to apologize. It's not your fault."

I nodded, though I knew he couldn't see me.

"I'm going to grab some candles and throw on something warmer."

I turned on my phone's flashlight and grabbed a hoodie from the closet, pulling it over my head before collecting the candles and flashlight.

Zach was still standing at the island, unpacking the food from the bags. I opened one of the kitchen drawers and pulled out a matchbook, lighting a candle and setting it on the counter away from anything it could burn. I took another one to the bathroom, put it on the vanity, and then placed the last one on the coffee table.

Thankfully, my apartment was small enough that there was plenty of light from the few candles I had. Everything was in the same room, aside from the bathroom, and since I left the door open, the light flowed out into the rest of the room.

"They gave us some paper plates if that works for you," Zach said, lifting the lids to the pizza boxes.

"That's perfect. Thank you. I'll give you cash for dinner."

"You will not," he replied sternly, handing me a plate.

I took it but placed a hand on my hip and shifted my weight.

"You can give me that look all you want, Andi. All it does is make me want to bend you over my knee and spank that tight ass of yours."

The look on my face changed in an instant as heat rushed through me. I turned away before he could see the blush on my cheeks.

"Now, get your food before it gets cold."

I debated answering him with *yes, sir,* but then worried he would probably like it, and I would likely get myself into something I couldn't get out of. It wasn't that I *wasn't* interested in Zach. It was that I knew he wanted to give this a chance, and I couldn't do a real relationship with him. A relationship wasn't on my radar right now, especially not after how my last one ended. If I had to pick between being with someone and going after my career dreams, I would always choose me—which was why I was still single.

I lowered my eyes and stepped in front of him as he guided me with a hand on my lower back.

My stomach growled loudly again as I grabbed a slice of the meat lover's pizza and pulled a breadstick out of the bag. I wanted to devour everything but didn't want to scare Zach off with my unladylike attack on the food.

I grabbed a few napkins and took my plate to the coffee table.

"Do you want a bottle of water?" I asked, opening the pantry door to pull them out. I didn't want to risk anything in the fridge going bad by opening it if I didn't have to. Plus, it was cold enough in the apartment that the water wasn't hot.

"Sure, that would be great. Thank you."

I grabbed two bottles and set them on the coffee table as he joined me on the couch with his food. I lifted the slice to my mouth and took a bite, the flavors exploding on my tongue.

"They have the *best* pizza," I moaned, closing my eyes.

"Indeed, they do."

I took another bite, trying to pace myself to enjoy it. The

warm glow of the light from the candles made it feel more romantic than it should have, and I hated that I didn't actually mind it at all.

"See, it's not so bad, is it?" Zach asked, wiping his mouth with his napkin.

"What isn't?"

"Dating me."

BLAME IT ON THE CANDY CANES

Twelve
Zach

My words lingered in the air as Andi avoided them. I didn't expect her to say anything, but then again, I couldn't help but hope that she was finally coming around to the idea.

If you would have asked me a month ago if I ever saw myself falling for Andi, my answer would have been no. But now that I had spent time with her in that capacity, my answer had quickly changed, and I found myself frustrated that it wasn't real by any means. I felt the chemistry between us, so how come she didn't?

"Would you like a dessert stick?" I offered, extending one to her.

She narrowed her eyes as she tried to find an easy way to take it from me without getting her hands covered in chocolate. They were delicious but messy.

"Open up," I offered softly as I scooted closer to her on the couch.

Her eyebrows raised slightly, but she didn't object as her mouth parted to accept the bite I offered. Her eyes closed as she chewed, a soft moan escaping her lips.

I swallowed hard and discreetly tugged at my jeans, desperately trying to hide the erection she was giving me.

Her eyes fluttered open as she opened her mouth for another bite, our gazes locking onto each other as I fed her. She blinked as she contemplated looking away but didn't. I gently pushed the last piece in between her lips, noticing the way they wrapped around my finger for a second before I pulled away.

"Sorry, I forgot how messy those are," she said behind her hand as she finished chewing.

"I don't mind messy," I admitted, bringing my fingers to my mouth and sucking the chocolate off them.

She watched my every move, her eyes hooded as she licked her lips, her breathing shallower than before. It was so fucking hot to see her react this way, and I wanted more. So much more.

"Do you want another one?" I asked, my voice gruffer than before.

She shook her head and reached her hand into the box, pulling one free.

"It's my turn to feed you."

My heart hammered in my chest as she scooted closer, her legs brushing against mine as she turned sideways on the couch and leaned in. Her delicate fingers brushed against my lips as she held the food between them, gently placing it in my mouth as I took a bite and chewed.

I could feel her eyes on me, studying my every move as my jaw worked tightly, fighting against the sexual frustration burning through me.

She lifted her hand for me to take another bite, the smell of chocolate floating around us. I grabbed her wrist and held it in place as I licked the food off her fingers. Her eyes locked on mine as I brought her fingers to my lips, sucking each one clean as if my life depended on it.

Her head tipped back slightly as another moan escaped her slightly parted lips.

I let go of her wrist and slipped my hand around the back of her head before bringing my mouth over hers. She gasped softly, but when I started to pull away, she wrapped her arms around my neck and climbed over, straddling me on the couch.

Our kiss deepened as she lowered herself down over my aching cock. Her fingers dug deeply in my hair, tugging gently while her hips rotated in small circles, grinding her body over mine. The heat rushed through my veins, my body alive from her touch.

My hands roamed over her body, grazing the sides of her breasts before lowering to her hips, guiding her movements. Her lips parted further, allowing my tongue access. Thoughts of her warm, wet mouth wrapped around my cock made it ache as my erection grew harder against my jeans.

"Andi," I panted, pulling away slightly, her lips moving to my jaw before kissing the side of my neck.

I dug my fingers into her hips, needing her to stop for just a moment.

"Are you sure you want to do this?" I pushed, needing to hear her say it.

"Yes."

"I need you to be clear on what you want, Andi."

"You, Zach. I want you to fuck me," she panted, sliding her

tongue up the other side of my neck.

I closed my eyes and grabbed her ass, desperate to get her pants off so I could really feel her.

Her lips met mine again as I lifted her hoodie up and over her head before tossing it to the floor. She was still wearing too much clothing, so I lifted her shirt and added that to the pile before rolling her off me and onto her back on the couch so I could take her pants off.

"You're so fucking beautiful," I said as I pulled them down her legs, taking in the sight of her wearing nothing but a black satin bra and matching panties.

"And you're wearing too many clothes," she answered, sitting up to unbuckle my belt as I grabbed the back of my shirt and pulled it off.

I rolled over and slid my jeans off, grabbing a condom from my wallet before tossing everything to the floor. I set it on the coffee table and then climbed on top of Andi as she lay on the couch, looking fucking incredible.

She reached up and wrapped her arms around my neck again, lowering me over her body as my cock poked through the fabric of my boxer briefs. I wanted to take my time pleasuring her before we did anything else, so I adjusted myself and began kissing down her body.

I made it to her stomach before I felt her grabbing at me, trying to pull me back up.

"I'm going to make you feel good, baby. I promise."

I lowered my mouth and continued my descent until I felt her press her legs together to keep me out.

I glanced up at her, trying to figure out what was wrong.

"Everything okay?" I asked softly, running my finger lightly over her skin.

"Yeah," she panted. "I just really want you inside of me."

I looked up and caught her eye.

"I want that too, baby. But I want to make you come first."

"Please, Zach. I can't wait. I need you inside me."

She pulled her lip between her teeth, desire heavy in her eyes. I nodded, understanding that she was feeling as aroused as I was and that there was time to make her come after we got our fill of each other first.

"Okay, baby." I met her eyes as I stood up and slipped my briefs off, stroking my cock as it sprung free.

"Shit," she whispered, staring at it in disbelief.

"Let me make sure she's ready for me," I offered, desperate to please her.

"She is. Trust me." She licked her lips but refused to take her eyes off my dick as I continued to rub it for her. "Please don't tease me any longer. I need that cock inside of me. Now."

I leaned down and hooked my fingers into her panties, pulling them down her body as her bare pussy glistened in the soft light.

"Fuck," I muttered, licking my lips as I ached to taste her. "You're shaved."

"I am."

I crawled on top of her, gently running my hand over her hip before sliding it over and grazing her pussy. She clawed at my back as I slid a finger inside, feeling her wet and ready for me.

I rubbed the wetness from between her lips onto her slit and then over her clit. She jumped against my touch, turning the corners of my lips into a devious smile as I leaned down and kissed her neck, desperate to taste as much of her as I could.

Her legs were tight beneath me as if she were fighting letting herself relax. I continued to fuck her with my fingers, loving how wet she was getting for me. My lips trailed over the satin of her bra before my teeth tugged the fabric down to expose a pebbled nipple. I pulled it into my mouth and sucked hard, loving how her body was reacting to me.

"Now," she whimpered. "Please, fuck me now."

I pulled my fingers out and lined up at her entrance after putting the condom on. I wanted to plunge inside and fuck her the way we both needed, but I wanted to feel her come first. I slid in slowly, allowing her to adjust to my size as she hissed through her teeth, her nails scratching down my back.

Once I was fully seated inside her, I began moving slowly, loving the way she gripped me tightly.

Her eyes closed as she tilted her head to the side and moaned, lifting her hips to meet mine as I sank deeper inside her.

I steadied myself, keeping the pace she liked while moving my thumb back over her clit and rubbing. Her breathing quickened, and I felt her legs tighten around me, which made me think she was close.

I rubbed faster, listening to her body and how it talked to me. But then suddenly, she lifted her hand and pressed it against my chest, her eyes wide open.

"Let's change positions," she said quickly, pulling as far away as possible.

"Okay," I stammered, unsure of what happened. "How do you want it?"

"Take me from behind," she said, moving as soon as I slid out of her.

She turned around and steadied herself against the armrest of the couch, pushing her ass up enough for me to enter, as well as giving me the perfect view of her tight, wet pussy.

I lined up again and pushed inside, closing my eyes as I tried to keep from coming right away. Just as I tried to reach around to rub her clit again, she moved her hips against the couch, blocking me.

I was frustrated that she kept making it hard for me to get her off, but once she started bouncing her ass on my cock, I lost it. I grabbed her hips, held her steady, and pounded into her until neither of us could take any more.

My balls tightened as I exploded deep inside her, my release filling the condom. I caught my breath for a moment, planting gentle kisses across her back as I slowly pulled out, making sure I kept my grip on the condom so it didn't spill.

I climbed down and went to the bathroom to deal with the mess, trying to hurry before she got dressed. I still wanted her to come, and now that sex was out of the way, she didn't have an excuse for not wanting me to.

By the time I opened the door a few minutes later, she was sitting on the couch, fully dressed again. I rubbed my lips together, unsure what to say, as I pulled my boxer briefs back on.

Her arms were wrapped around her waist, and I couldn't tell if it was a protective mechanism against me or if she was that cold. With the power being out and the storm raging outside, it was hard *not* to be cold in here. There was no way I was going to let her stay here tonight. She would freeze her ass off.

 "Grab your stuff, and let's get going," I said as I stood up and grabbed my clothes, getting dressed while she watched.

"Go where?"

"You're staying with me tonight," I said matter-of-factly as I pulled on my hoodie.

"No, I'm not," she said with a laugh. "I'm fine here, thank you very much."

I took a few steps toward her and noticed how her eyes automatically went straight to my cock. Sure, my groin was technically lined up with her face, but still, I was more than a piece of meat.

"My eyes are up here, Andi," I teased, lifting her chin with my finger. "Now go pack a bag, and let's get going. You're not staying in an apartment with no heat."

"You're not the boss of me," she said defiantly, lifting her chin and pulling away from my touch.

"Okay, fine. Have it your way."

The cutest look of confusion crossed her face right before I bent down, threw her over my shoulder, and carried her to the closet, where I packed a bag for her.

Thirteen
Andi

I had no clue what to say after Zach acted like a wild caveman and took me to his house. At first, I was going to protest, but the way his hands grabbed my ass as he held me over his shoulder had me strongly reconsidering. I'd already had a taste of Zach, and now I wanted more.

The ride to his house wasn't as awkward as I thought it would be. We were quiet the entire time, with Zach acting like nothing happened as he tapped his fingers against the steering wheel and belted out Silent Night with the radio. I was worried that he didn't have power either until we walked inside, and I spotted the fireplace in the dim light from his phone's flashlight.

"We'll sleep in my bed tonight," he said, pointing to the king-sized bed in the center of the room as he continued the tour of his house, showing me where everything was.

It was bigger than I would have imagined, though I couldn't say I had any expectations to begin with.

"I'm not sleeping in your bed," I scoffed, wrapping my arms around my middle.

"Why not?"

"Because…" I knew there was a reason this was a bad idea;

I just couldn't figure out what it was.

"Andi, I've already been deep inside you. I don't think we need to worry about sleeping together tonight, especially since it will involve actual sleep."

My cheeks flamed from his words, and I looked away, walking into the large bathroom attached to the master bedroom. He shone the light over my head so I could see everything, but I stopped in my tracks when I spotted the giant soaking tub.

"Feel free to use it. I have a gas water heater, so you don't have to wait for the power to come back," he said softly, standing behind me as his hand grazed my lower back. He lit a few candles on the vanity by the sink.

"Thanks," I breathed, suddenly overly impacted by his touch.

I stood there for a few minutes, staring at it as if it were the most magical thing in the world.

"Are you coming?"

I looked over to find humor dancing in his eyes from his play on words.

I wish.

I followed him out of the bathroom and into the bedroom, where he tossed some wood into the fireplace and got it going. I sat on the edge of the bed, my body already sinking into the plush mattress as waves of exhaustion washed over me.

"How about sleep first, soak later?" he asked as if reading my thoughts.

"Sounds like a plan." I stood up and grabbed the bag he

packed for me, noticing there weren't any pajamas in it.

"Looking for something?" he asked over his shoulder, a smirk playing at his lips.

"Yeah, it seems someone forgot to pack pajamas." I lowered the bag and tilted my head to look at him.

"I didn't forget."

"Okay, then where are they?" I pulled open the bag, looking again.

He stood up, tossed another piece of wood into the fire before closing the gate, and then came to where I was standing.

"There aren't any pajamas in there."

"Why not?"

"Because I couldn't stand the thought of having you sleep beside me wearing layers of clothes."

I attempted to lick my lips, but my mouth was dry, and it was hard to swallow.

"Oh," I whispered.

"You can sleep in one of my T-shirts if you'd like."

"What about bottoms?" I asked, looking up to find his blue eyes locked on me.

"You don't need them."

"What if I get cold?"

We stood chest to chest, the heat between our bodies hotter than the fire.

"As your boyfriend, it's my job to make sure this beautiful pussy of yours never gets cold." His hand gently brushed against my groin, his fingers sliding across my slit.

"*Fake* boyfriend," I hissed, trying to get the words out as my eyes closed and I leaned into his touch as he rubbed me right where I was aching.

"Trust me, Andi. There won't be anything *fake* when you're with me. Relationship or orgasms—just so we're clear."

He rubbed his finger harder against my clit and then pulled away, my body sagging against him.

"I'll give you a moment to get changed," he said, planting a kiss on my forehead.

I already missed the heat from his body as he moved away, stepping into his closet to pull out a shirt. He handed it to me and then walked out, giving me a moment to gather myself.

I changed quickly, stripping off my bra and pulling on his soft t-shirt. I kept my leggings on, knowing I would be cold without them. Once I was done, I headed down the hallway and found him in the kitchen. His back was to me as he reached into the cabinet, his shirt riding up a tad, showing off a perfectly sculpted torso.

I leaned against the wall and watched, feeling the rush of heat between my legs again. I couldn't help it; Zach turned me on in so many ways. I wanted to let him show me how easy it would be for him to make me come earlier, but I knew deep down that it wasn't that simple. I'd never been able to achieve climax, even by myself, so the last thing I wanted to do was embarrass myself with Zach by not coming like I should. I had gotten used to rushing through sex and faking it when I had to, but for some reason, I didn't want to do that with Zach.

It was like he knew me better than any of the guys I'd dated before. Maybe I was worried he would call me on it if I faked an orgasm with him, which he probably would. But I couldn't wrap my head around the idea of him being able to get me there. That would be too good to be true, and I was scared to let myself get my hopes up that he would be the one to change things for me. I was used to disappointment but didn't want to have it with Zach. That was why we couldn't treat this as a *real* relationship. We could have sex and have fun with our *fake* relationship until my parents went home, but that was it. Everything had to end there.

"How do you like the shirt?" he asked over his shoulder, somehow knowing I was there even though I had been quiet as a mouse.

"It's perfect," I answered. "Super soft and comfy."

"Good. Though I was going to say you could go without it if you didn't like it. I wouldn't mind." He lifted a bottle of water to his lips as he smirked.

"I'm sure you wouldn't," I laughed. "But it wouldn't seem fair that I have to sleep naked while you get to wear pajamas."

"Oh, I don't wear clothes when I sleep," he said, pushing off the counter he was leaning against and handing me an unopened bottle of water.

I giggled at the thought of him sleeping naked and took it, allowing him to lead me back to his bedroom.

"Where do you want me?" I asked, not sure where to put my water down.

"Is that an offer?" he joked, wiggling his eyebrows. "Because if so, I'd definitely like to have you face down, ass up in my bed. But then again, I would love to fuck you in the shower or have you ride me in the tub. Maybe have you ride my face once we're done. The choice is yours." He shrugged.

"I meant *to sleep*," I laughed, shaking my head. "Where do you want me *to sleep*?"

"I'm guessing *on my cock* isn't the answer you're looking for?"

"No." I shook my head again, trying not to let the smile grace my lips.

"Fine, pick a side," he laughed, running a hand down the stubble on his jaw.

"But which—"

"Just pick a side, Andi. I'll sleep wherever. Stop overthinking it."

I nodded and went to the side that looked like it had fewer personal belongings on the nightstand. I set my water and ChapStick down, feeling weird not having a bunch of stuff cluttered on there like I had in my studio apartment. That was the problem with small spaces; you always lacked the space you needed.

I pulled the blanket and comforter back and started to climb in when I heard him clear his throat on the other side of the bed. I looked over to find him in nothing but his boxer briefs, removing his watch as he nodded to my leggings and shook his head.

"You're kidding, right?" I laughed and put my hands on my

hips. "I'm going to be cold without pants."

"And I told you, it's my job to keep you warm."

He came up behind me and wrapped an arm around my waist while nudging my head to the side with his before kissing along my shoulder. My body immediately began to melt against his, the tension in my shoulders dissipating.

His fingers hooked into the waistband of my leggings and began lowering them, moving slowly as he kissed his way down my body. He moved around to the front as I stood before him, wearing nothing but his t-shirt and a pair of panties.

"These too," he whispered gruffly, taking his time removing my panties.

I stepped out of them, noticing how his face was lined up between my legs.

"Can I taste you?" he asked softly, looking up at me, his blue eyes pleading.

I chewed my lip nervously and then nodded.

He tossed my underwear to the side and shifted his body so his shoulders lined up with my hips. My fingers dipped down and tugged on his hair as my head fell back at the first swipe of his tongue against my slit. I hissed out a breath, desperate for more.

It was hot and warm and fucking incredible as he continued to tease me with his mouth. When he started sucking my clit, I felt that initial tingle in my spine and knew we needed to stop. It would only lead to disappointment when he got me to the brink of coming, only to have it not happen. I would end up a hypersensitive bundle of nerves with no release and frustration for days.

"You taste so good, baby," he murmured loud enough for me to hear him. "I want nothing more than to keep eating this pussy. Is that okay?"

I moaned as he slid a finger inside, spreading the wetness across my skin.

"Fuck," I moaned, starting to press my legs together and forcing his head out.

"Come for me, baby," he coaxed, gripping the back of my thighs with his hands as he tried to open them again.

My mind immediately flooded with thoughts and worries about being unable to come, forcing me out of the moment. I chewed the inside of my cheek in frustration, debating whether to have him stop and risk having to explain what happened or to give in and fake it.

His finger began pumping inside me again as his tongue flicked my clit rapidly. But it was useless. The tease of an orgasm from a few seconds ago was gone.

Hating myself for what I was about to do, I grabbed a handful of his hair and tugged hard as I faked coming. I moaned and cried out his name, trying to make my body do the things I thought it should do during an orgasm—not that I'd ever had one to go off of.

"Fuck! Yes! Right there, Zach," I cried out, pressing his head harder against my pussy. "Ahhhhh!"

I clenched my muscles down there a few times for good measure, expecting to see a look of satisfaction on his face as he looked up at me. Instead, there was a frown.

I could feel the heat wash over me in waves as he stood up and lifted my chin to force me to look at him.

"You fucking faked that."

Fourteen
Zach

Andi was unusually quiet on our way to work this morning, though I knew why. After I called her out on faking an orgasm last night, she shut down and didn't have much to say. We went to bed, and I held her body against mine, following through on my promise to keep her warm. But other than that, nothing else happened.

This morning, I hadn't been able to stop overthinking last night and trying to figure out where I had gone wrong. I could feel her body reacting to me and knew her orgasm was building. It was obvious with how her muscles tightened around my fingers. But just when I thought she would let go and have a mind-blowing orgasm, it was like it just vanished from her body, and I got fake Andi instead.

I wasn't mad—okay, that's a fucking lie. I was angry that she faked it with me, but only because I thought we had a better relationship than that. Not that we were technically dating, but because we had been friends for a while, and I thought she could trust me. Obviously, I had been wrong about that.

Once at the shop, Andi checked on the items I prepared yesterday, making sure the backup generator had held up throughout the night. Thankfully, the power came back on in the middle of the night, and the worst of the storm had passed, so it was unlikely that the power would go out again anytime soon.

"I'm going to head over to Sugarplum Lattes," I said, needing an excuse to get some fresh air. "Do you want your usual?"

"Yes, please." She walked over to her desk and pulled out her wallet.

"I got it," I said, holding my hand to stop her.

"No, it's my treat."

"Andi," I warned, folding my arms over my chest. "Put your money away. I don't want it."

She inhaled deeply and forced it out in a heavy sigh.

I knew better than to stay and fight with her, so I turned and walked out, pulling my beanie over my head to ward off the chill in the air. It was a short walk to Sugarplum Lattes, and thankfully, they had already been out to clear the sidewalk.

It was busy inside, but that was the usual, given it was the only real coffee shop in Sugarplum Falls. I waited in line, trying *not* to think about Andi while I waited to place my order. Christmas songs played softly over the speaker as lights twinkled from the ceiling, creating the perfect ambiance. I still needed to help Andi get the giant inflatable elf up outside, but thankfully, the inside was decorated a few weeks ago. You couldn't live in Sugarplum Falls and *not* decorate. It was basically a sin, and everyone made sure you knew it.

Finally, I was up and made my way to the counter.

"Large peppermint mocha latte with extra whipped cream and a large salted caramel cold brew?" Sam asked, his fingers hovering over the keys on the register.

"You got it. Thank you." I slid my debit card to him and looked around, hating that I wasn't feeling talkative like usual.

I stepped to the side and waited for the coffee while people bustled around me.

"Here you go," Sam said a few minutes later, handing me the to-go cups in a tray.

"Thanks." I smiled and took it from him, noticing the look in his eyes.

"Hold on a minute," he said, bending over to grab something from beneath the counter. "Here, two candy canes."

"Um, thanks." I held them up and smiled again.

"My grandpa used to say they were the key to lovers' quarrels. By themselves, they're just candy canes, but put them together, and they make a heart. Sometimes, all it takes is a step back, a good cup of coffee, and something to remind you of the love you have for each other."

"Oh, I… Um." I shoved a hand through my hair, unsure of what to say. "That's not. Andi and I aren't."

He grinned as he studied me, waiting for me to be able to form a sentence.

"That's not what this is," I said, nodding to the coffee and shaking my head.

"You sure? Because I've been noticing a change between you two lately."

"We're um… It's complicated." I sighed heavily, shifting my weight.

"Love usually is. Enjoy the coffee." He winked and then went back to helping with the line.

I walked out feeling unsure about what had just happened. If Sam thought something was going on between Andi and me, then everyone else had to be thinking the same, too. I made my way back to the shop and went inside, ready to distract myself with today's orders.

"Are you guys dating?" Liv asked quietly, though loud enough for me to hear through the small window up front.

"It's complicated," Andi answered in a hushed tone, not knowing I was on the other side of the door, hearing everything.

"Why? You guys are like *sooo perfect* for each other."

"What?" Andi laughed. There was a lot of movement in the kitchen, and if I had to guess, I would say that she was getting stuff set up to start on the pastries before we opened this morning.

"You are! Everyone thinks so. We've all been waiting for you two to get your heads out of your butts and realize it too."

"People are talking about us?" Andi questioned nervously.

"Not in a bad way," Liv assured her. "More of a —*we knew this was coming, so why are they still hiding it* kind of way. But then again, I only get so much gossip as the assistant manager. They could be saying more, I don't know."

"Wow. I honestly didn't see that coming."

"So, you guys are dating then?" Liv pushed.

"Um. Yeah. We're dating."

"I knew it!" Liv exclaimed, fisting the air in triumph. "I

could see that coming from a mile away."

"Shhh!" Andi scolded.

"What? We're not even open yet. No one else is here."

I stood on the other side, eavesdropping as I debated trying to sneak out so I could come back in louder.

"Zach will be back any minute," Andi warned.

"Does he want it to stay a secret?" Liv asked.

I knew Andi didn't talk to many people about her personal life, but she and Liv were friends outside of work, so it didn't surprise me that they were having this conversation.

"I don't know. We haven't talked about it. I'm sure he would be fine with people knowing, but I'm not ready yet."

"Why not?"

"I don't know," Andi sighed heavily. "I guess I just don't want to rush things right now. Things are going well, and if everyone knows about us, then there's this new pressure I don't want to deal with. I'm his boss; what happens if we break up? Is he going to up and quit?"

"I seriously doubt that," Liv replied. "But I think if things are going good, don't worry about what could go wrong. Live in the moment and enjoy what you have. And not to be rude—but I would *seriously* enjoy that if you know what I mean."

"Liv!" Andi laughed, the sound filling the room.

"What? I'm just saying that I've seen him knead dough, and that man seriously knows what to do with his hands. I wouldn't complain if he wanted to have some secret love affair with me."

"You're so bad. And married!"

"Yeah, but you like it, and I would never act on it. Just saying that I've noticed some *talent*."

I heard footsteps and started to panic, heading back to the front door before they spotted me.

I quietly opened the door and stepped out, pushing it open again right as Liv came through the doors from the kitchen to the front.

"Good morning, Liv. I didn't know you were going to be here this morning."

"I decided to come in and help get caught up on orders. Plus, my in-laws are in town and staying with us, so I needed to get out of the house for a while."

I laughed, knowing how much she *enjoyed* their visits.

"I grabbed coffee for Andi, but I can run back and grab something for you if you'd like," I offered, setting the tray on the counter separating us. She looked down, spotted the two candy canes, and smiled.

"Sam told you about the candy cane story?" she asked, still grinning.

"Yeah," I sighed.

"Well, don't let me keep you. In fact, I think I'll go ahead and walk down to grab some coffee myself. Give you two a few minutes."

She winked, grabbed her coat from the rack, and walked past me. I wasn't sure if she knew I had heard everything they said, but I didn't bother to ask her.

I grabbed the tray and pushed through the door, finding Andi at the counter with the supplies she needed set out in front of her. I set the tray down harder than I intended, some of the coffee splashing out of the tiny holes in the lid.

She looked up at me in surprise, startled by it.

There were so many words I wanted to say, but none of them would come out. I leaned in, grabbed her by the waist, and pulled her into my chest. She gasped softly and then immediately relaxed in my arms. I lowered my mouth to hers and kissed her the way I had wanted to all morning. This didn't resolve the *fight* we were still having, but that didn't matter right now.

BLAME IT ON THE CANDY CANES

Fifteen
Andi

The day flew by faster than I had imagined, and I was thankful once it was over. Between Liv and I, we got a lot accomplished and were able to get slightly ahead for the week. Tomorrow would be a long day with staying late to get the sugar cookies done for the Frosty Fest, but thankfully, Liv was able to find a couple of high school kids who could come help out this week. With the extra hands up front, I would be able to pull Becky and Denise to the kitchen to work on orders while Zach helped me with the sugar cookies. There was a lot to get done, but I felt confident that we could do it.

"Are you ready to go?" Zach asked, leaning against my door.

"Yeah. You?"

He nodded and shoved his hands into his pockets.

I closed the windows on my computer and turned it off, then grabbed my cell phone and shoved it into my purse. Zach already had his hoodie and beanie on, watching me slide into my peacoat and wrap a scarf around my neck.

We walked out, and he waited while I locked up. The snow was still thick around my car since it was in a shaded part of the parking lot and hadn't had a chance to melt in the freezing temperatures today. I groaned quietly and pressed the button to open my trunk so I could grab the shovel.

I pressed it again and again. Nothing. I walked over, unlocked the door, and sat down to start the engine. Only, it wouldn't start.

"You've got to be kidding me," I grumbled, resting my forehead on the steering wheel.

"Battery is dead," Zach said, standing beside me, tucked into the space between the door and my seat.

"Can you give me a jump?" I asked, attempting to climb out as he continued to stand there.

"Come home with me," he blurted out.

"What?"

"Come home with me. We can deal with this tomorrow. It's already late and cold."

"I'm fine. If you can just give me a jump start," I said wearily.

"I could, but then your battery would be dead again tomorrow morning, and you'd have to wait for me to come jump you again. No one is open right now, Andi. It's going to have to wait until tomorrow anyway."

"Ugh." I leaned back in defeat.

"Just come home with me. It's not like you haven't stayed already. You can sleep in one of the guest rooms if you want. Use the soaking tub."

I could hear the desperation in his voice to get me there, but I was reluctant to go because I knew what would happen if I did.

"I don't know," I sighed.

"I don't want to keep going caveman on you unless you're really into it, so if you could get out and come willingly, that would be great. If not, I'm two seconds away from throwing you over my shoulder and hauling your ass out of here before I freeze my balls off."

"Alright. Alright. I wouldn't want to be responsible for your frozen balls." I pulled the key out of the ignition and got out.

Zach closed the door behind me and placed his hand on my lower back as he guided me to his truck. He helped me in and then went around and climbed into the driver's seat. I fastened my seatbelt and tried to assure myself everything would be fine. There wouldn't be any awkward conversations about what happened last night or the fact that he knew I had faked it.

We pulled up, and I felt a smile creep onto my face as I took in how beautiful his house looked lit up with white Christmas lights. I didn't know what to expect from Zach, but this wasn't it. He came around and opened the door, extending his hand to help me out.

"The lights look beautiful," I said, still in awe.

"Thank you. The woman I hired did a wonderful job."

"You hired someone to do this?" I asked, letting him guide me to the front door with his hand gripping my elbow to keep me from slipping on the ice beneath us.

"Yeah, I was running out of time and had no idea what to do. This is the first year I've had my own place, so I asked around, and Shelly came highly recommended. I'm impressed with how much she was able to get done today."

"Well, she did a great job."

He unlocked the door and held it open as I stepped inside. The house looked different than it did this morning, probably because I was grumpy and we were rushing to get out the door and to the shop. I took in the floor-to-ceiling windows in the living room, noticing the large tree decorated in the corner between them.

I walked over and looked at the ornaments, each one a white snowflake of a different shape and size, leaving none of them to be the same.

"That was the only request I had when she did the tree," he said, standing beside me as we stared at it. "That each ornament be a snowflake."

"They're beautiful," I commented softly. "I love that none of them are the same."

"Just like real ones."

I smiled and kept my attention on the tree instead of focusing on how my body felt so close to his.

"Are you hungry?" he asked, still staring straight ahead.

"A little."

"You didn't eat lunch today," he pointed out. "I imagine you're more than a little."

"How do you know I didn't eat lunch?" I asked, turning toward him.

"Because I know everything about you, Andi."

He turned and headed to the kitchen, leaving me to follow behind him.

"What can I help with?" I asked, lingering by the door instead of joining him at the island.

It was a beautiful kitchen with stainless steel appliances and marbled countertops. Dark gray wood floors brought everything together and made the cream-colored cabinets pop. I hadn't noticed any of these details this morning, so it was like I was seeing everything for the first time.

"I got it, but thank you."

"I don't mind helping," I insisted. "If you have milk and cereal, that's fine with me. I'm not picky and don't need a fancy meal."

He bent down and pulled a skillet from a cabinet beneath the island.

"I'm making chicken parmigiana."

"Oh," I said, surprised that he knew how to cook that. "How do you kno—"

"How do I know it's your favorite?" he interrupted, catching my eye before opening the fridge to pull out a pack of chicken. "Because, Andi, I know everything about you. I know that you always order chicken parmigiana on payday for dinner and that you substitute the angel hair pasta for fettuccine noodles because you like that they're thicker. I also know you get an extra order of breadsticks because you like to dip them in the sauce before piling noodles on top and taking a bite. I also know that you prefer to drink Moscato with it, but you only do it at home because you worry that people will judge you for drinking a sweet wine with dinner."

I opened my mouth to speak but snapped it shut when I didn't know what to say. I was going to ask how he knew how to make it, wondering if maybe his mom cooked a lot and he learned from her. But I was surprised to hear just how much he knew about me without me noticing before now.

"Go soak. Dinner will be ready in an hour. The wine is chilling in the fridge."

I nodded and backed out of the kitchen, heading to the tub.

My head was still spinning with what Zach said as I filled the large tub and sprinkled in some Epsom salts. There was an assortment of bath products on the ledge of the tub against the wall, but I felt bad for using them. It wasn't like they were mine, and based on the look of them, some of them looked like they might have belonged to a girlfriend at some point.

The tub continued filling, steam fogging the mirror as I stripped off my clothes and got in. My body ached as the hot water enveloped me, quickly soothing away the pain. I dipped lower, allowing my shoulders to be submerged, knowing that was where most of the tension was built up.

I closed my eyes and leaned my head back against the soft bath pillow, wondering how often Zach took advantage of using his tub. If I lived here, I would never get out. I would spend all of my free time here, soaking my worries away.

There was a soft knock on the door before it opened. I sat up quickly, trying to move the water around to keep him from seeing me naked in the water.

"I brought you a glass of wine," he said, extending it to me. "And don't worry, I've already seen you naked, Andi. No need to try to hide from me now."

"Thank you," I replied quietly as our fingers brushed. I took a sip and then set it down on the ledge, ignoring the jolt that ran through me from our contact.

"Enjoy your bath." He turned and walked out, leaving me a flustered mess of emotions.

I sank deeper under the water and tried to drown out my worries for just a few minutes.

<u>Sixteen</u>
Zach

"How's your food?" I asked, ignoring the way my cock was pressing into my jeans every time Andi moaned around each bite.

"It's delicious, thank you. I had no idea you could cook like this," she admitted, hiding her mouth behind her napkin as she finished chewing.

"There are a lot of things I can do." I pinned her with a look and watched the blush creep across her skin.

She lowered her head and twirled the pasta around her fork before taking another bite.

I wanted to circle back to the fake orgasm thing last night, but I wasn't sure how to approach it. There was something between us that I wanted to explore, but I couldn't if she was going to hold back from me. Unlike what people may have thought about me, I didn't just fuck any girl who came my way. I was selective in whom I was intimate with, and I expected there to be a level of trust and open communication between us.

We continued eating in silence, the only noise being the sound of our silverware clinking against the plates or wine glasses being set on the table. Suddenly, Andi's phone rang, startling both of us.

"It's my mom," she said, looking down at the caller ID.

"You can take it if you want."

She pressed the button on the side of the phone to silence it and slid it to the side.

"It can wait."

My lips pulled into a thin line as I attempted to smile.

There was still an awkward tension between us, and it was driving me crazy.

Andi lifted the breadstick to her mouth, the sauce dripping down the side of it. Her tongue darted out, catching it as she licked up the side of it.

"If you keep doing that, I'll give you something else to lick," I warned, gripping my fork a little too tightly.

Her eyes widened as she looked from the breadstick to me.

"Feeling a little jealous of a breadstick?" she teased, holding it inches from her face, her fingers moving to grip it the same way I imagined she would hold my cock before sucking it.

"No," I lied, shifting under the table.

"So it wouldn't bother you if I did this?" she asked, bringing it to her mouth as she parted her lips and ran her tongue down the side of it.

"Not at all."

"Well, something must be triggering you," she mused, chewing her lower lip. "Maybe it was this?"

She locked eyes with me as she opened her mouth and slid it inside, slowly closing her lips around it before pushing it in with one finger, nearly taking the whole thing down her throat.

"Fuck it," I growled, slamming my fist on the table. I pushed away, tossing my napkin to the side of my plate as I quickly crossed the space between us. Her eyebrows shot up as I grabbed the end of the breadstick and pulled it out, tossing it on the plate as she stared at me in disbelief.

"You want to play games?" I asked, clearly not amused. "Fine. Let's play."

"What are—"

I grabbed her by the waist, tossing her over my shoulder before carrying her down the hallway to my bedroom.

"Zach!" she shrieked, giggles escaping along with it. "What are you doing? I wasn't done eating!"

"You want something to eat? You can suck this cock like you were that breadstick."

"Don't you dare threaten me with a good time," she warned, the desire thick in her voice.

She reached down and grabbed a handful of my ass, squeezing hard. I smirked and shook my head before slapping her ass, knowing there would be a beautiful red mark to greet me as soon as I got those damn leggings off.

I dropped her to the bed and quickly worked to remove her clothes.

"Have I told you how much I like this whole caveman thing?" she asked, leaning back on her elbows as I removed her pants and panties in one quick swoop. Her legs parted slightly, showing me her wet pussy.

"You don't have to. She's saying everything I need to hear." I winked, lifted my shirt over my head, and tossed it to the side.

Andi looked incredible laying in my bed, and while I wanted to see her completely naked, I didn't want to waste any more time so I could finally eat her out. I slid up her body, planting kisses along the inside of her thighs until I reached the sweet spot I wanted so badly.

I positioned myself between her thighs, holding them between my arms to keep her from pushing me away again. Her pussy was already wet, begging to be played with as I leaned in and slid my tongue along her slit.

She hissed out a breath and arched her back, making me grin with satisfaction. I was determined to make her come this time and ignored my throbbing cock that desperately wanted a turn inside her.

I went slow, taking my time as I played with her, not bothering to use my fingers since I needed to hold her legs open. She trembled against my touch, moaning softly each time I slipped my tongue between her folds and fucked her with it.

Her breathing increased more rapidly, and I knew she was getting close. I focused on her clit, flicking it quickly with my tongue before pulling it between my lips and sucking hard. She cried out, her fingers gripping the sheets beneath her.

I gripped her thighs tighter as I continued sucking, determined to get her off this time.

"I need you to fuck me, please," she whimpered.

I ignored her pleas and continued with my mission.

"Zach," she groaned, pulling strands of my hair to get my attention. "I want your cock. Now."

I didn't have to ask if she was still close to coming because

I could feel it in her body. The tension that had built up a few minutes ago suddenly disappeared.

I pulled my head out from between her thighs and looked up at her, a million questions on the tip of my tongue.

"How do you want it?" I asked, frustrated that I hadn't gotten her off again. I rolled off the bed, stripped off the rest of my clothes, and laid beside her.

"However you do," she panted.

"No, Andi. How do *you* want it? Tell me what you want." I lazily stroked my cock, smirking as her eyes followed the movement.

"I want to ride you." Her eyes moved up and caught mine. "Is that okay?"

"Fuck yeah," I growled, laying on my back so she could climb on. "You can ride whatever you want. My cock. My face. Whatever you need to get off, Andi."

Her cheeks turned the cutest shade of pink as she rolled over and straddled me.

"There are condoms in my drawer," I said, nodding to the nightstand.

She pulled it open and grabbed the box, frowning when she opened it.

"It's empty."

"What?"

I popped up on my elbows and frowned.

She turned it toward me, showing the empty contents inside.

"Fuck," I groaned, shoving a hand through my hair as I laid back and closed my eyes.

She set the empty box back on the nightstand, the movement of her skin brushing against mine, making my cock twitch.

I wanted to be inside her so bad, and she was literally inches away. All it would take was one slight move, and I would be sliding through her wet slit. Her tight pussy welcoming me in a warm embrace.

"I'm on the pill and just had a physical a few months ago. I'm clean," she offered, chewing her nail nervously as my cock rested between her ass cheeks.

"I'm clean too. I get checked every year. The last one was six months ago, and I haven't been with anyone besides you since then."

She grinned and lifted her hips before reaching back and gripping my dick.

"Then it looks like that's settled," she whispered as she lined me up at her entrance and hovered over me.

"Just one thing real quick," I said, opening the drawer to my nightstand and bringing out the candy cane vibrator I won at the party. "Candy Cane gets to play tonight."

She giggled as I turned it on, the vibration sound increasing as I pushed the button to where I wanted it. I lined it up at her clit as she slowly slid down onto my cock.

"Shit," I hissed, grabbing her hips and digging my fingers into her flesh with one hand while holding onto the vibrator with the other. "Fuck, Andi."

"You feel so good," she moaned, sliding slowly down my length, taking me as deep inside her as she could.

"You too, baby. So fucking good."

She moved her hips, grinding against me in the most incredible way. I gripped her hip tighter, trying to prolong coming until she decided to lean forward slightly and let my cock rub against her clit as she rode me, pushing the vibrator out of the way. If she wanted my cock to get her off instead of a toy, that was fine by me.

I closed my eyes and tried to regulate my breathing so I could give her time to get off before I did.

She panted heavily as she continued to ride, clenching her pussy tightly around me with each thrust.

"Come on my cock," I instructed, opening my eyes to watch her.

"I want you to fill my pussy," she said, grinding her hips faster, sending me straight over the edge.

I wanted to protest and demand that she come first, but I couldn't hold off any longer. I dug my fingers into her hips and held her in place as I lifted my pelvis and thrust hard and fast into her. My cum shot deep inside her, slowly dripping down her legs by the time she pushed off and I slid out.

She rolled over next to me and closed her eyes as we both caught our breath.

I waited a few seconds before I was going to ask her why she wouldn't let me make her come, but instead, was interrupted by her cell phone ringing in the kitchen. I laid there with frustration mounting again as she climbed out of bed to deal with whoever was calling.

BLAME IT ON THE CANDY CANES

Seventeen
Andi

The next few days had flown by in a flash. Between it being our busy time of the year at Sugarplum Sweets and taking on the custom order for Jasmin for the Frosty Fest, I was struggling to keep my head above water.

Zach and I hadn't talked much about what happened the other night in his bedroom, probably because I was avoiding talking to him as much as possible. I was pretty sure that everyone had already figured out that we were "dating," given the looks people gave us whenever they saw us together. I hadn't stayed at his house the past few nights, but only because I was so exhausted from working double shifts to get ahead on the cookies that I insisted on going to my apartment so I could get some actual sleep. Being at his place meant we would find ourselves sleeping together, and neither of us would be rested. However, that hadn't stopped me from tossing and turning all night, wanting to feel his presence next to me.

Sam had been sending over handfuls of candy canes every time we picked up our drink order, which seemed odd, but I didn't have time to think about it. It was after two on Friday, and I was in the final stretch of finishing the cookies before I had to deliver them tomorrow morning for Frosty Fest.

My hand cramped from gripping the frosting bag while I worked on decorating the Santa sugar cookies. The kitchen was bustling around me as everyone worked on getting the orders out up front while I stayed in my corner, out of the way.

"Son of a bitch!" I muttered when a giant blob of white icing shot out, covering Santa's face.

I slammed the bag of icing down and looked around for the knife I had been using to fix errors as they happened.

"What's wrong?" Liv asked, approaching the metal table with two to-go cups from Sugarplum Lattes. She set the tray down and leaned forward to see what I was working on. "Oh my God! It looks like Santa got a—"

"Don't you dare say it," I warned, pointing the knife at her.

"Alright, alright," she laughed, holding her hands up.

"What's with the candy canes?" I asked, noticing two on the tray tucked in between the cups.

"They're from Sam."

I arched an eyebrow and looked up under my lashes while trying to get the icing off without ruining the rest.

"What's his deal? Is he like obsessed with peppermint or something?" My tone was snarky, but I was tired, my feet were killing me, and I couldn't figure out why he kept sending so many candy canes my way.

"They're for your lovers' quarrel." She smiled softly.

"My what?" I set the knife down and stared at her, giving her my full attention.

"His grandpa used to tell him that the key to solving a lover's quarrel was to sit down, have a cup of coffee, and eat candy canes. By themselves, they're just candy canes, but put them together, and they make a heart."

"I don't get it." I shook my head, brows pinched together. "He thinks you and me are fighting? Or that we're lovers?"

"It's not you and *me*." She looked over her shoulder to Zach. "He picked up your coffee order. Not me."

"How does Sam know about—"

"The same way Sam remembers what I ordered on my wedding day. The same way he knows what your favorite drink is or how many shots of espresso you like when you're having a bad day. He pays attention. He has a gift for picking up on things we might not even see ourselves."

She smiled and shrugged before heading back up front to deal with the store while I contemplated that for a moment.

I felt Zach's eyes on me as he wrapped an apron around his waist to get back to work. I smiled and looked away before anyone noticed. I grabbed the coffee from the tray with my name on it and took a big sip, letting the peppermint mocha sooth my nerves. I let the caffeine work through my body and returned to decorating the cookies.

By six o'clock, everyone was wrapping up for the day and the last orders had been picked up. Next week would be busy as well, with it being the last week before Christmas. This weekend was not only the Frosty Fest but a handful of holiday parties, which most of our orders had been for. Next week would be filled with smaller orders and less bulk ones, like pies and pastries for Christmas Day.

I pulled out the metal stool from under the table and sat down, my feet aching as much as my back. Most of the cookies had already been boxed up for tomorrow, but I still had a few dozen I needed to finish now that the frosting had dried.

"Want some help?" Zach offered, heading into the kitchen from the break room.

"Na, I'm fine," I lied, forcing a smile to my lips.

He leaned against the wall and crossed his ankles while he stared at me.

"Why do you do that?" he asked, his voice low.

"Do what?" I stood up and grabbed a stack of boxes from behind me that still needed to be assembled. It was going to be hours before I got out of there at this rate. My body was too tired to move quickly.

"Lie to me."

My head whipped up to find his eyes locked on me.

"I'm not lying to you. I'm fine. I knew this order would be a lot of work and that it would mean late nights."

"You're not fine, Andi," he exhaled heavily, pushing off the wall to crowd my space. "I know you better than that, so I'll ask again."

"Okay, fine," I laughed nervously, holding my hands up to stop him from pressing further. "I'm tired, but that doesn't mean I'm lying. I don't need help, but thank you for the offer."

He was standing too close, the smell of his cologne intoxicating. It reminded me of being tangled up in his bed sheets and licking the sweat off his chest as he pounded into me.

He shook his head and arched an eyebrow at me before pulling out another stool and sitting beside me.

"Give me some of those," he said, nodding to the stack of boxes.

I knew it was pointless to argue with him, so I divided the stack in half and passed him some.

We worked quietly, assembling the boxes faster than I would have been able to do on my own.

"Thank you for your help," I said quietly, not looking up as I pushed the side in and folded the flap to hold it together.

"You're welcome."

My phone rang in my pocket, interrupting the peace and quiet I finally had in the shop. Zach kept working while I pulled it out and groaned when I saw my mom's name on the caller ID.

"Hey, Mom," I said, pressing the phone between my ear and neck so I could finish my box.

"Hey, sweetie. I was calling to see if you and Zach wanted to go to dinner tonight."

"Thanks for the offer, but we're still at the shop finishing an order for the Frosty Fest tomorrow. Maybe another time?"

"You've been saying that for a week," my mom said dryly.

"Yeah, well, I've been busy this week. I told you how hectic it gets this time of year," I replied tensely, hating that I had to defend myself again.

"I know, but it would be nice to see you every now and then while we're in town visiting."

"I'm sorry, Mom." I sighed heavily, switching the phone to my other ear. "Maybe we can grab dinner tomorrow night instead?"

"I thought you had Zach's holiday party tomorrow night?" she questioned.

I closed my eyes and pinched the bridge of my nose. I had completely forgotten about that little lie.

"Oh. Yeah. You're right. *Zach's family holiday party* is tomorrow," I said through gritted teeth since I knew he was listening. I didn't want him to decide now was a good time to pipe up and volunteer us to do something with my parents.

"I'm surprised you forgot, given how adamant you were about not being able to attend the Hendricks' party because of it."

"I didn't forget, Mom. I've just been busy and focused on work. I can't see past today, so it just slipped my mind that it was this weekend, that's all."

"Well, it would be nice to see you guys while we're here. You've already said that you're busy with work next week too. Is there ever going to be a time when we get to hang out with you? We did travel all this way—"

"I know," I snapped, starting to lose my cool. I had explained how busy I would be *before* they booked their trip here, so it wasn't fair that she was giving me grief about it when she knew in advance. I knew that the whole purpose of the trip was to spend the holiday with me, but it didn't make it any easier for me to just *free up* some time.

Zach gently grabbed my hand, squeezing it to get my attention. He motioned for me to give him the phone, clearly having heard everything my mom was saying, given that she spoke rather loudly.

"Hold on for a minute, Mom." I covered the mouthpiece with my hand and looked at him. "What are you doing?"

"Just trust me, okay?"

I eyed him suspiciously and then passed him the phone.

"Hi, Jen," Zach said smoothly, completely relaxed beside me. "I know it's last minute, and I apologize for that, but my parents asked that you and Ross join us tomorrow night if you're available."

He nodded while my mom said whatever she was saying. I tried to listen but couldn't hear anything past the ringing in my ears.

"Absolutely. It'll be just the six of us, a cozy and casual event."

He paused, his grin spreading ear to ear as my mom responded.

"Wine would be wonderful, thank you. I'll have Andi send over the information as soon as we get out of here. I look forward to seeing you guys tomorrow at the Frosty Fest. Be sure to stop by our booth. I'll have some of my famous snowballs."

I shook my head, wondering what in the world had gotten into him.

"Perfect. Thanks, Jen. Have a great evening."

He passed the phone back to me, still smirking as I looked to see that my mom had hung up.

"What was that all about?" I asked, bewildered.

"I invited your parents to my parents' holiday party tomorrow night."

"Why would you do that? There's not even a party!"

"I guess there is now." He pulled his cell phone out of his pocket, pressed a few buttons, then held it to his ear. "Hi, Mom. We're having a dinner party at your house tomorrow night."

I pressed the palm of my hand to my forehead and tried to focus on anything other than the room spinning around me.

<u>Eighteen</u>
Zach

The line to grab coffee this morning was insane with everyone getting ready for the parade. I had helped Andi get the cookies to Jasmin before everything started, then left to grab us lattes while Andi and Liv worked on setting up the booth for Frosty Fest.

Thankfully, everything except for the parade took place inside the mall, so no one was stuck in the blistering cold. Sugarplum Sweets had one of the largest booths, and our team had busted their butts yesterday to prepare for today. Basically, we took what we made for a typical day at the shop and tripled it. Frosty Fest was THE place to be, and we wanted to ensure we were prepared without selling out by midday.

I finally made my way back with three lattes and a peppermint stick for Andi's coffee. It was like Sam had an intuition to know when things were off between me and Andi. This time, he didn't give us the regular candy canes he'd been sending with our order. Instead, it was just the stick, which I assumed was for Andi to stick in the cup for extra peppermint flavor.

"Good morning, Liv," I said, sneaking into the back of the booth and pulling her drink from the tray. "Here's your vanilla latte."

"Thank you so much," she replied, her eyes filling with tears as she took it. "That was so thoughtful of you."

"Not a problem," I assured her as I dug out Andi's and handed it to her. Thankfully, I had spotted Liv coming in as I was heading out to get the drinks, and Sam knew her order. But then again, why wouldn't he? He knew everyone's.

"Sam sent a peppermint stick over as well," I said, handing it to Andi.

"Oh, thank you." She furrowed her brow and then laughed before tucking it into her back pocket. "Sam sure does like his peppermint."

Liv and I didn't bother commenting on that and helped with setting up the rest of the boxed cookies and cupcakes instead.

There were boxes upon boxes stored beneath the tables, each lined up under the item on the table for easy access when we needed to refill. There was an assortment of pastries, decadent chocolates, and sugar cookies galore, which were all guaranteed to sell out in no time.

I worked on setting up the tasting station, where we had a small sampling of everything for those who wanted to try before buying. It seemed silly to me, given that everyone in Sugarplum Falls had been to Sugarplum Sweets at least once—if not hundreds of times already. But it made sense to have it out, just in case someone was on the fence and needed to be sure before purchasing.

Finally, everything was done, and we had time to sit down for a second before the doors opened and people started filing in, heading straight to our booth. I grinned when I

She shrugged and put back the ornament she was looking at. She walked around to the other side of the table, looking at the more festive ones while I grabbed the white pearl cross one she had held onto for so long and snuck it under the one I was buying for the party.

Once we were done, we stopped by a few more booths so I could finish up some of my holiday shopping. I didn't want to keep Andi out too long since she was so tired, but she seemed to get some energy every time we stopped at a new booth.

"What time is the party tonight?" she asked as we walked to my truck.

"Dinner is at six, but I told my parents we would be there a little early."

"Okay," she said, nodding as she waited for me to open the door and help her in. I didn't bother looking away as her dress rode up, showing me her creamy thighs that I wanted to be in between.

"So, what do your parents think of this whole thing?" she asked once I got in and started the truck.

"What do you mean?"

"You know, the whole *fake dating* thing."

"I didn't tell them." I looked at her over my shoulder, noticing her brows pulled together.

"Why not?" she demanded, her tone turning angry.

"Why would I?"

"Because if not, they'll think we're really dating," she said gruffly.

"And what's wrong with that?"

"Well, we're not dating, for starters," she huffed.

"Yeah, but everyone else, including your parents, thinks we are. Why would we do anything different with my parents?"

"I don't know." She threw her hands up. "I guess I just assumed you had explained it to them, and that's why they agreed to throw this party to help with our lie."

"Nope. My mom *loves* parties, so it wasn't a big deal when I asked her to throw one."

"She didn't ask any questions about why you invited me and my family?"

"I told her that you and I were dating and things were getting pretty serious, so we wanted our families to meet since your parents were in town."

"You didn't." She closed her eyes and leaned her head against the headrest.

"I did."

"You shouldn't have done that," she groaned.

"Why? What's the big deal? People in relationships meet each other's families all the time, Andi."

"Yeah, but we're not in a relationship, Zach. You've just made it that much harder to break up with you."

I pressed my tongue into the side of my cheek because there was no way I could deny I did that on purpose.

saw Andi pull her shoulder's back, take a deep breath, and handle it like the pro she was.

There was a lot of chatter as people huddled closely, trying to see what was available and grabbing for boxes of treats before someone else grabbed it. Liv, Andi, and I worked our asses off, moving around each other effortlessly as if we had done this a hundred times.

"Can you hand me some boxes of the turtle truffles?" Andi asked, looking down as I grabbed a few boxes of sugar cookies to replenish my side of the table.

"Sure. Let me grab them."

I leaned forward, my arm brushing against her leg as I reached for the stack she needed. She had on a red, fitted dress that looked festive and showed off her legs with the black heeled boots that went over her knees. There wasn't much space in the booth for anyone to see her, but as I tried to maneuver beneath her, I couldn't help but think about how close her pussy was and how badly I wanted to taste it.

 I grabbed the stack and pulled them out, bonking my head on the edge of the table as I climbed out.

"Are you okay?" she asked, panic in her voice as she looked from the customer in front of her to me.

"Yeah, fine. I was just distracted, that's all."

She blushed as if she knew exactly what had distracted me.

"Here you go," I said, handing the stack to her.

"Thank you."

I smiled and looked around the table, checking to see what

else needed to be replenished. Andi and Liv had somehow worked out getting people to form two lines instead of crowding the table, which allowed me to be helpful by grabbing whatever they needed and bagging orders.

"Why, Andi, this is just incredible!" Jen said, taking the open spot in Andi's line. "Look at this, Ross. Our baby girl is the busiest booth here! People are lined up to get her treats!"

"Well done, Andi," Ross said, leaning in to kiss her cheek.

"Thanks you guys. I'm glad you came to check it out. There are a lot of great vendors here, so be sure to check them out, too."

"We will, dear. But first, I came to get some of Zach's famous snowballs," Jen said, rubbing her hands together as she spotted me.

"Oh, um, I don't think we have any," Andi said, scanning the tables around her.

"I brought them special for you," I replied, resting my hand on Andi's lower back as I reached down and grabbed the box I had made for her parents. "Here you go."

"Oh, these look delightful!" Jen's eyes widened as she studied the coconut truffles, then turned the box so Ross could see.

"You're a sneaky one," Andi teased quietly, turning her head so only I could hear.

"We'll take a box of assorted fudge, sugar cookies, and two boxes of cupcakes."

"Mom, what do you need two boxes of cupcakes for?" Andi laughed, grabbing a bag to start loading the boxes in.

"Well, one is for us to enjoy in our rental, and the other is for the party tonight. I think the ornament ones would be perfect."

Andi gave me a look, then grabbed the cupcakes for her parents and handed them to me. I bagged everything up while Andi fought with her parents about letting them pay for their stuff.

"Hey, sorry I'm late," Becky said, squeezing in behind me. "Janice and Delta should be here in a few minutes so you guys can get out of here and take a break."

"Sounds great, thank you."

I took a few minutes to show the afternoon crew where everything was, pointing out the low stacks so they knew that was all there was once it ran out. Liv was staying the entire day and had told Andi she needed to leave at noon and take the rest of the day off. She tried to object but stopped when we all gave her *the look*.

"That line is insane," she commented, gathering her stuff as we squeezed out of the booth. "I should stay and help them."

"They've got it," I assured her. "You need to take a break. Plus, there's some shopping we need to do before tonight."

"Shopping?" Her eyebrows raised, and I could see how exhausted she was with the bags under her eyes.

"It's not a lot, but yes, we need to buy a few things for the party."

"Okay, just tell me what to do."

I tried to keep the look off my face, but when her cheeks flushed, I knew she had seen it.

"Let's head to Sugarplum Gifts. They'll have what we're looking for."

I grabbed her hand and led the way, hoping her boots weren't killing her as she struggled to keep up behind me.

Their booth was busy but not as bad as Sugarplum Sweets had been, so thankfully, we didn't have to wait too long before we got to the table where racks of ornaments were hanging.

"We're doing an ornament exchange tonight," I said, holding a white furry star one in my hand. "Pick your favorite."

"They're all so beautiful. It's hard to pick just one," she replied softly, already lost as her fingers brushed over the delicate ornaments in front of her.

"Then pick a few."

"But we only need one each, right?"

"Yeah, but I'll buy you the other for your tree."

"That's very sweet of you." She smiled and looked up at me. "But I don't even have a tree."

"You don't have a tree?!" I asked a little too loudly, earning curious looks from those around us. "How do you not have one? That's like a sin, Andi."

"Shhh," she scolded, looking around and lowering her head. "It's not like I have room for one, and I live by myself. Why go through all the effort of putting one up when I'm the only one who will see it."

"Because it's Christmas. Everyone should have a tree at Christmas."

She shrugged and put back the ornament she was looking at. She walked around to the other side of the table, looking at the more festive ones while I grabbed the white pearl cross one she had held onto for so long and snuck it under the one I was buying for the party.

Once we were done, we stopped by a few more booths so I could finish up some of my holiday shopping. I didn't want to keep Andi out too long since she was so tired, but she seemed to get some energy every time we stopped at a new booth.

"What time is the party tonight?" she asked as we walked to my truck.

"Dinner is at six, but I told my parents we would be there a little early."

"Okay," she said, nodding as she waited for me to open the door and help her in. I didn't bother looking away as her dress rode up, showing me her creamy thighs that I wanted to be in between.

"So, what do your parents think of this whole thing?" she asked once I got in and started the truck.

"What do you mean?"

"You know, the whole *fake dating* thing."

"I didn't tell them." I looked at her over my shoulder, noticing her brows pulled together.

"Why not?" she demanded, her tone turning angry.

"Why would I?"

"Because if not, they'll think we're really dating," she said gruffly.

"And what's wrong with that?"

"Well, we're not dating, for starters," she huffed.

"Yeah, but everyone else, including your parents, thinks we are. Why would we do anything different with my parents?"

"I don't know." She threw her hands up. "I guess I just assumed you had explained it to them, and that's why they agreed to throw this party to help with our lie."

"Nope. My mom *loves* parties, so it wasn't a big deal when I asked her to throw one."

"She didn't ask any questions about why you invited me and my family?"

"I told her that you and I were dating and things were getting pretty serious, so we wanted our families to meet since your parents were in town."

"You didn't." She closed her eyes and leaned her head against the headrest.

"I did."

"You shouldn't have done that," she groaned.

"Why? What's the big deal? People in relationships meet each other's families all the time, Andi."

"Yeah, but we're not in a relationship, Zach. You've just made it that much harder to break up with you."

I pressed my tongue into the side of my cheek because there was no way I could deny I did that on purpose.

Nineteen
Andi

"What are you wearing?" I asked, covering my laugh behind my hands as I opened the door to Zach. He stood on the other side wearing a reindeer onesie and looked ridiculously cute.

"My Christmas pajamas." He shrugged and held out a bag to me. "I brought you yours."

"What?" I giggled, still not able to get over him with the hood pulled up to show off the antlers.

"It's a pajama party." His grin spread across his cheeks as he extended the bag to me again. "We gotta hurry, though. I told my parents we'd be there by 5:30."

I took the bag and looked inside to find a matching reindeer onesie.

"How did you know what size to get?"

"It was easy."

"Because you *know everything about me*?" I teased, stepping back and holding the door open for him to come in.

"No. The sales lady was pretty much the same size as you, so I just asked what size she would get and went from there."

I shook my head and laughed, impressed by his resourcefulness.

"You didn't need to do this, but thank you. If you would have told me it was a pajama party, I could have grabbed something myself."

"Yeah, but if I told you that, you would have found some boring, plain pajamas, and I would miss out on seeing you in a reindeer onesie."

"That's very true." I laughed, pulling it out of the bag and holding it in front of me. "I'm gonna change real quick."

He sat on the couch and pushed his hood off, still looking silly in his outfit. I went into the bathroom, closed the door, and got dressed.

I was surprised that it was the perfect fit, given that he went based on what size another woman wore instead of asking me. But I also appreciated the surprise element and that he kept me from being a Grinch and not participating, which we both knew was likely had he told me in advance.

I turned in the mirror, checking out the outfit before touching up my makeup and adding more blush to my cheeks to play it up. I pulled the hood over my head and opened the door, prancing out playfully.

Zach stood up and came over, giving me a quick twirl as he took me in.

"I don't think I've ever said this before, but I seriously cannot wait to tap that reindeer ass later," he growled, pulling on the short tail on my butt.

"Well, behave and maybe you will." I scratched my nails softly against the scruff dotting his jaw, then stepped away to grab my purse and phone.

I felt nervous on the way to his parents' house, but hearing Zach sing along to Christmas songs on the radio instantly soothed my nerves. His voice was amazing, and the way he sang with so much soul and conviction had me admiring the man beside me.

We pulled up to a gorgeous house decked with Christmas lights hanging from the roof and wrapped around the shrubs and trees. A giant inflatable Santa and Mrs. Claus stood in the middle of the yard, waving to those who passed by.

I waited for Zach to open the door and help me down, my stomach in knots again.

As we walked to the door, we held hands, already putting on a show as a happily involved couple. I hated lying to his parents as much as I did with mine, but we were in too deep now to stop. Breaking up a week before Christmas would be enough to fuel the town gossip for months and break our parents' hearts, ruining Christmas.

I pulled my shoulders back, took a deep breath, and adjusted my hoodie so the antlers stood up right as we heard voices on the other side of the door.

"Welcome! Welcome!" A beautiful woman wearing an elf onesie greeted us, stepping to let us in as a man in a matching onesie joined her.

"Mom, Dad, this is Andi," Zach said, introducing us as we entered the house. "Andi, this is my mom, Pearl, and my dad, Daniel."

"We know who Andi is," Pearl laughed, pulling me in for a hug. "We've only been going to Sugarplum Sweets every chance we get since you started working there."

His mom swatted at his arm before pulling him in for a hug and to plant a kiss on his cheek.

"Right," Zach laughed, tipping his head back and closing his eyes in embarrassment. "Sorry, I've never had to do this before."

"Well, I personally am not upset with you bringing a girl home for the first time," Pearl said. "Especially it being sweet Andi!"

She pulled me in for a hug as Zach and his dad greeted each other.

"It's so wonderful to have you here, dear. What a blessing it is that you and Zach are together. I swear, I was just telling Dan that this might be the best Christmas gift we've ever gotten. Heck, maybe the greatest gift ever!" she squealed, releasing her hold on me.

I tried to smile, but her words went straight through my heart and burned.

"Andi, it's so nice to see you again," Daniel said, leaning in for a casual hug. The kind you give when you don't really know someone and don't want to make them uncomfortable, which I appreciated more than he could know right now.

"Go ahead and set your stuff down. The ornaments can go on that table," she said, pointing to where two gift bags were already sitting. "I have eggnog ready, but if you want something different, we have a full bar ready as well."

"Eggnog is great, thank you," I murmured, trying to clear my head and be back in the moment.

His mom and dad went to the kitchen to get our drinks as we set our bags on the table next to theirs.

"You okay?" he asked quietly, his hand splayed across my lower back.

I shook my head, struggling to take the breath I needed to refill my lungs.

"What's wrong?"

"Your mom thinks this is the greatest gift she's ever gotten," I whispered sternly, not looking up to meet his eyes.

"So?"

"So?! It's a lie, Zach! She's going to be so hurt when she finds out the truth." I scrubbed my hands down my face. "I didn't think about how many people we would hurt when this came to an end when I first proposed it. I'm screwing everything up."

He reached over and grabbed my hands, lowering them to my waist.

"Who says we have to break up, Andi?"

"That was part of the plan. We agreed this would be a fake relationship until my parents left, and now everything is getting out of control. All because I didn't want to risk being set up." I shook my head and inhaled deeply, not bothering to let it out.

"What if this has nothing to do with that?" he questioned with a tinge of anger in his voice.

"What are you talking about?" I snorted; of course this had everything to do with not wanting to be set up. If I hadn't been worried about that, none of this would have happened to begin with.

"I'm serious, Andi. I keep saying this, and you keep shutting it down. What if this isn't about you being set up, and is fate and the universe bringing two people together because they're *meant to be together*."

"I—"

"Eggnog is ready," Pearl said, interrupting us as she brought two cups in.

"Thanks, Mom," Zach said, taking them and handing me one.

"Your dad is watching a movie in the living room if you want to join him. I'm going to go finish dinner before Andi's parents get here."

"Can I help?" I offered quickly, desperate to get some space from Zach.

It wasn't that I didn't want to be around him; I just couldn't allow myself to consider what he was saying right now. One of us had to stay clear-headed, and it needed to be me.

"Sure, dear. Right this way."

I smiled and followed Pearl to the kitchen while Zach joined his dad in the living room.

Pearl pulled a pan of roasted potatoes out of the oven and gave them a toss with the spatula before returning them and shutting the door.

"The chicken is roasting, the potatoes are almost done," Pearl said more to herself than me. "All that is left is the salad and bread."

"Well, feel free to put me to work," I said awkwardly, holding my hands in front of me.

"Thank you, dear. If you want to make the salad, that would be wonderful."

I smiled and waited for her to pull everything out of the fridge, then got started washing and cutting the vegetables. We worked together in silence, which was wonderful for me because I was worried I would end up slipping and blurting out that this whole thing was fake and ruining dinner.

Ten minutes later, the doorbell rang, and Pearl set the sliced bread in a basket on the table and rushed off to answer the door. I took a few steadying breaths and wiped my hands on a kitchen towel before following her out.

"Hi, I'm Jen, and this is my husband, Ross," my mom said as she and my dad stood in the entryway, greeted by Zach's parents.

I stood to the side, giving them a few minutes to introduce themselves as Zach stood next to me, wrapping his arm around my waist. I looked up at him, brows pulled together before remembering we were supposed to look like a happy couple. I forced the scowl off my face and leaned into him, allowing the steady sound of his heartbeat to sooth me.

Zach's parents moved aside, and I burst into laughter when I spotted my parents' pajamas.

"Oh my gosh," I squealed, holding my hands to my cheeks. "You guys look amazing!"

"Thanks," my dad said, leaning in to hug me. "It was your mom's idea."

My dad wore a pink bunny onesie, like the one from *A*

Christmas Story, while my mom wore black pajamas with a gold skirt over them, resembling the lamp from the movie.

"We've had so much fun picking out all of these costumes for the different parties we've gone to," my mom gushed, following Pearl into the house.

We sat at the dining room table, and Pearl brought out the rest of the food while Daniel filled everyone's glasses with wine. My parents instantly connected with Zach's, and we sat back and watched as if they were best friends who had known each other forever.

My dad was in the middle of telling everyone about the Hendricks' party when Zach leaned over and whispered in my ear.

"See, I told you there was nothing to worry about."

He squeezed my leg gently beneath the table, but I was more worried now than I had been before.

Twenty
Zach

We sat in the living room, enjoying a cup of hot chocolate while we all let our full bellies settle. My mom loved to cook, so it was no surprise that she had made enough to feed an army. On top of that, Andi's parents had brought a handful of baked goods that we had been snacking on since.

Andi was cuddled into my side on the couch while our parents laughed and told their favorite holiday story. It was a tradition that my parents did every year, though it was usually on Christmas Eve before we would open one present and then go to bed. I knew they were doing it tonight as a way to include Andi and her parents in something special our family did. It was like they were in this for the long haul and setting building blocks to expand our family.

"My favorite holiday memory was Christmas of 2008," Jen said, smirking as she looked at Andi and lifted her mug to her lips.

"Noooo, Mom. Please don't tell that story," Andi groaned, pulling a throw pillow out from beneath her and covering her face. "It's so embarrassing."

"Oh, no. We've got to hear it now," I teased, tickling her sides until she dropped the pillow. She giggled and leaned into me, making my heart still for a moment as I realized there was nothing fake about what I felt for Andi. I knew I was falling for her, I just hadn't realized how hard until now.

"Well, Andi was eight," Jen continued, locking eyes with her daughter.

"Why do you hate me?" Andi pouted, her lower lip plump and begging to be kissed.

"There's no hate, dear," Jen laughed. "I can't help that it's my favorite holiday story."

"Mine too," Ross said, giving Andi a wink.

"Anyway," Jen cleared her throat. "Andi was eight, and they had built these beautiful gingerbread houses in school. She was so excited to show us when she came home that day. It was a few days until Christmas, so I told her to set it on the table where we would put the pies on Christmas Eve. I had been so busy that I hadn't noticed that every day, she was taking a few pieces of candy off of the house and eating it. By Christmas Eve, the house was completely bare. I had wanted to use it as a decoration, to show it off to our friends and family at our annual Christmas Eve party, but Andi ate most of it before I could. She figured since it was on the dessert table, it was for eating."

"I didn't know any better," Andi said, pulling her hood on to try to cover her face. "I had never made one before. I didn't know you weren't supposed to eat them. Why would they give kids that much candy and then tell them not to eat it?"

I tipped my head back and laughed.

"Do I need to watch you at the shop?" I teased.

"No," she said, swatting at me playfully. "I don't eat them *anymore*."

"Are you sure? Because come to think of it, I did notice

a few of the decorations had been missing recently." I pressed my finger to my chin and tapped it.

"That wasn't me! It was the kids from the toddler decorating class!"

"Mmm hmm, sure it was. Blaming the innocent kids for your gingerbread house candy addiction."

She narrowed her eyes but couldn't stop grinning as she tried to elbow me in the side. I caught it and pulled her closer instead.

"That's a cute story," Mom said, smiling at Andi and her parents.

"What about you, Andi? What's your favorite holiday story?"

She shifted next to me and gave it some thought.

"I don't know. That's a hard question. I think it would have to be a few years ago, the last Christmas we had with my grandpa before he passed. He loved Christmas, and he always decorated his house to the nines. I think that's why it felt so natural to move to Sugarplum Falls and be surrounded by people who love it as much as he did."

"But you don't even have a Christmas tree up in your apartment," I objected, drawing everyone's attention to me by accident.

"So," she said through gritted teeth, elbowing me hard in my side.

"Andi Rose, you haven't put a tree up yet? It's a week until Christmas!" Jen exclaimed.

"There's no room in my apartment for one," Andi said, narrowing her eyes at me.

"That's no excuse," her mom continued. "They have small trees that fit on your table. You can get one of those, and I'll come over and help you decorate it."

"That's not necessary, Mom. Really. Thank you, though." Andi turned and pinned me with a look. "Why don't we have *Zach* tell us his favorite holiday memory?"

I knew she was putting me on the spot to get back at me for outing her about not having a tree up. Little did she know, I had already been thinking long and hard about my favorite one while everyone else shared theirs.

"Easy," I said, rubbing the palms of my hands down my onesie. "This Christmas is my favorite because I get to share it with the woman I love."

Andi's eyes widened as she stared at me, taken aback by what I just said. Our parents oohed and ahhed while Andi and I shared a moment I never wanted to let go of.

Twenty-One
Andi

He said he loved me.

It wasn't like it was a joke and everyone laughed at the punchline. No, he admitted to our families that he was in love with me. That *I* was his favorite holiday memory.

After that, I pretended to be getting tired—which wasn't really pretending because I was exhausted from the past week. But I needed an excuse to cut the night early and go home. I needed to be away from Zach and his love and having to wonder if he meant the words he said or if he was just playing the part for our families.

We gathered around the coffee table, playing a game for the ornament exchange. Every ornament that was opened was beautiful, and I loved how tears formed in my mom's eyes when she picked the one I had purchased at the festival. It was an angel with feathery white wings holding onto a gift. When I picked it earlier, I pictured it as the angel delivering a gift to my grandpa in heaven, which was the same thing my mom had said when she clutched it to her heart.

Pearl had picked the snowman with rosy red cheeks and a carrot nose, while Daniel went for the Santa one that had him hanging off a roof, the bottom half of the ornament separate from the top so it could swing to make him look like he was falling. My dad chose the blue and silver star because it reminded him of the Dallas Cowboys, his favorite football team, leaving Zach and me to pick last.

I hadn't seen what he bought because he had already paid while I was still looking. Zach was next to pick, which meant I would get the last gift bag and whatever ornament was inside. By the looks of it, there were no losers because all the others were gorgeous—not that I had a tree to hang it on anyway.

He looked between the two bags, which was funny, given that one was the bag he brought with his ornament. He grabbed the other one and pulled out a gold heart-shaped frame ornament.

"I think I have the perfect photo to put in this," he said, winking at me.

I had no idea what he was talking about, but I smiled and played along. Just a few more minutes and then we could leave—or I could call for a cab and let him enjoy some time with his family.

He wrapped the ornament in the tissue paper and tucked it into the bag.

"Your turn," he whispered, nudging me with his arm.

I smiled, even though it was still forced, and grabbed the last bag on the table. I could feel everyone's eyes on me as I unwrapped the layers of tissue paper and pulled out the pearl cross ornament I had fallen in love with earlier. I ran my fingers over the front, tears pooling in my eyes.

"How did you—"

"I saw how much you loved it earlier."

"Thank you," I whispered, my words getting stuck in my

throat. "I guess it was luck that I ended up with it after all, huh?" I laughed, holding it in my hand.

"I like to believe it was fate," he replied, pinning me with a look.

Everyone began talking around us before getting up to refill their drinks, leaving us to our moment. Once we were alone, he turned to face me.

"Are you ready to get out of here?" he asked softly, rubbing his finger across my cheek tenderly.

"Yeah. Sorry, I think this week is catching up with me. I can call a cab, though. That way you can spend some time with your parents."

"I'm not letting you take a cab home, Andi."

"Why not? I'll be fine," I insisted, standing up.

"Because you're my girlfriend, for one."

"*Fake* girlfriend," I whispered, checking to make sure no one was close enough to hear.

"Two, it's my responsibility to make sure you get home."

"Bu—"

"Not only do I know that I don't *have* to, I want to. Please do not fight me on this."

"Okay," I conceded, too tired to argue.

We said our goodbyes and left, both laughing at how well our parents had hit it off. They hugged us and then returned to the conversations they were having as if they had known each other for years.

I climbed into Zach's truck, buckled up, and leaned into the seat as my eyes felt heavy. The exhaustion washed over me in waves, and soon, I was lulled to sleep by the low hum of the engine as he drove.

"We're home," he said softly, gently shaking my arm to wake me.

My eyes fluttered open as I looked around, trying to figure out where I was.

"Let's get you to bed."

"You could have taken me to my apartment," I murmured, struggling to unbuckle myself.

He reached over, pressed the button, then got out and helped me down.

"I wanted you to get a good night's sleep."

"What makes you think I won't get that at my place?" I asked, looking up at him as he unlocked the door and pushed it open for me to enter. I yawned, covering my mouth.

"Because you seem to be better rested the mornings after you've stayed with me."

"That's not true," I objected through another yawn.

"Yes, it is."

"Alright, Mr. I Know Everything," I muttered sleepily as I shuffled into his house and eyed the couch. It looked comfortable enough to pass out on.

"Nope. I don't think so." He spun me around and guided

me down the hall to his bedroom as if reading my thoughts.

I was way too tired to do anything but pass out.

"I know I usually have the no pants rule in bed," he teased with a cheeky grin. "But since you're technically already wearing pajamas, I won't make you take them off."

"Thanks." My eyes teared up as another yawn took hold of me.

He pulled back the covers and climbed in behind me, wrapping his arms around my waist as he pulled me into him. Feeling his muscular body against mine made me feel safe and cared for as I drifted to sleep.

BLAME IT ON THE CANDY CANES

Twenty-Two
Zach

I never thought I would wake up wrapped around a sexy reindeer, but there we were. Andi shifted, rolling onto her side as her hand grazed against my crotch. I groaned quietly, the combination of morning wood and Andi in my bed making my dick want some action.

"Good morning," she murmured sleepily, strands of red hair covering her face.

"Good morning indeed." I leaned in and kissed her forehead, always loving the moments when I got to wake up with her in my bed. "How are you feeling this morning?"

"Like I could sleep the day away. What time is it?"

I poked my head up to see the clock on the nightstand.

"It's after nine."

"I never sleep that late." She rolled over and brushed the hair out of her face before looking up at me.

"I told you, you sleep better here."

She grinned, but I could tell something was weighing heavily on her mind when it didn't reach her eyes.

"I think we need to talk about last night," she said quietly, pulling out of my arms and sitting up against the headboard.

I swallowed hard, already knowing I wouldn't like where this was going.

"Sure," I replied as easily as I could. "What's up."

She inhaled deeply, shoulders pulled back, then slowly released it as she turned to face me.

"While I appreciate everything you've done for me with this whole fake relationship thing, I don't want you to feel like you have to keep doing all you're doing."

"What do you mean?" I asked. I knew what she was getting at, but I needed to hear her say it.

"You know what I mean," she sighed, throwing her hands in the air. "The whole being in love thing. You don't have to keep pretending that we are."

I looked into her eyes and held her gaze.

"Who says I'm pretending."

The color on her face drained quickly as we continued to stare at each other. I was laying it all on the line with her right now because I needed her to know that I wasn't just pretending. Along the way, I fell for her.

"Zach," she whispered.

"I know I wasn't supposed to fall for you, Andi, but I did. And I won't apologize for it because fake dating you has been better than anyone I've ever real dated."

She leaned her head into her knees and hid her face.

"You weren't supposed to get feelings," she said softly, lifting her head as tears filled her eyes.

"Tell that to my heart."

"I think it's time for me to go." She refused to look at me as she climbed out of bed and rushed to the bathroom, closing the door behind her.

I leaned back against the headboard and closed my eyes. This wasn't the way I wanted this to go.

Twenty-Three
Andi

I didn't talk to Zach again after he dropped me off at my apartment yesterday. Things were awkward and uncomfortable between us, but thankfully he had today off, so I didn't have to worry about that interfering with stuff at work.

We still needed to talk and figure out when we would tell our parents that we had broken up. I wanted to wait until after Christmas but knew that was no longer possible. I couldn't continue to go on and pretend like we were in love when he was starting to have real feelings for me. That wasn't fair to him and I shouldn't have put him in this position to begin with.

I knew it would ruin Christmas for both families with the break up being so fresh, but it was better than forcing ourselves to spend it together and making it awkward for everyone. This was what needed to happen; I just had to keep reminding myself.

"Do you think we have enough truffles?" Liv asked, standing in front of the table I was working at that was filled with them.

"I want to make sure we have enough," I muttered, not bothering to look up.

"Or you're stress baking."

"I do not stress bake."

"You're so full of shit," she said, chuckling as she pulled a stool out and sat down. "So, what happened?"

"What are you talking about?" I glanced at her, noticing the sadness on her face as she watched me.

"With you and Zach. What happened?"

"Nothing. It's over. He's fine. I'm fine. Everything is fine."

"Except that it's not."

"Why can't you just accept that it is?" I blew out, setting the spoon I was using hard on the table as I looked up and glared at her.

"You've made five dozen truffles this morning, Andi. We don't even sell that many in a day. We're going to have to put them on sale just to go through the inventory you've created."

I pulled my head back and looked down. She was right. I had been so focused on *not* thinking about Zach that I didn't notice how many I had made.

"Shit."

"It's fine. I'll jump on social media later and post a Holly Jolly sale. People love those."

"Thanks," I muttered, lowering my head and shaking it.

"So, what's going on? Talk to me."

"Nothing." I shrugged. "It's over."

"But why? You guys seemed so happy."

"Things changed. I don't really want to talk about it," I said softly, lifting my eyes to look at her.

"Okay," she said, standing and pushing the stool back under the table. "I'm here if you need me. Just promise me one thing?"

"What's that?"

"Don't bake anything else today. We're good. We have plenty to get us through the next few days. Spend some time in your office if you need to, or leave early and finish some Christmas shopping. Just please, for the love of God, don't bake anything else."

Her cheeks split into a grin that had the corners of my mouth pulling up, too.

"Deal."

She went back to the front, so I cleaned up my mess and asked Delta and Becky to handle packaging up the truffles for Liv. I went to my office but couldn't focus, so I decided to take a long lunch and finish my Christmas shopping.

I was browsing the aisles at Waldon's, looking for something else to get Liv, when I turned the corner and ran into my parents.

"Mom, Dad," I said, trying to get my heart to stop racing after almost running my cart into theirs. I had been so lost in thought that I hadn't noticed them. "What are you doing here?"

"Just some last-minute shopping. We wanted to get a few things for Pearl and Dan since they'll be coming for Christmas dinner. I figured we can wait and open presents after dinner if that works for you?"

I knew my parents had rented a house while they were here so they could host Christmas dinner like they always did, however, I didn't expect the additional company. My throat burned as I tried to get the words out, my hands gripping the shopping cart's handle a little too tightly.

"Um, I don't think that's necessary," I said with a shake of my head.

My mom's eyes narrowed as she set a scented candle in the top of her cart and tilted her head to study me.

"Why not? It would be rude to have them over and not have a gift to give them. You know better than that."

"I know, Mom," I stuttered, suddenly hating that I had to do this. I lowered my eyes, not wanting to see the hurt on their face when I told them we had broken up.

"Andi, what's wrong?" Dad asked, setting his hand on my shoulder.

I rubbed my lips together, the words not coming.

"I um… It's… Well…"

"Honey, what's going on? I haven't seen you this tongue-tied since you were in that school play and couldn't remember your lines." Mom's tone was gentler, but I knew she would be devastated as soon as I told her.

"Zach and I broke up," I spit out, snapping my mouth shut as soon as I did.

My mother's head pulled back in surprise, looking stunned by the news.

"Oh my," she whispered. "I can't say that I saw that coming." She held a hand to her heart.

"I'm sorry," I said quickly. "Sometimes things just don't work out."

I gripped the handle, ready to get the hell out of there.

"But you were so happy, Andi. Are you sure it's over?" Her eyes pleaded with me to give her hope.

I nodded and looked around, not wanting to look at her as I broke her heart.

"Sometimes you just have to talk things out. Get to the bottom of whatever is causing a rift between the two of you. Good communication is the key to a great relationship, honey. Have you tried that?" she asked.

My heart raced as my blood pressure skyrocketed. I tipped my head back and blinked rapidly to keep the tears from forming in my eyes.

"It's not that easy, Mom."

I chewed the inside of my cheek, trying to take the pain away that I felt so deeply in my chest.

"Love is never easy, dear."

"We're not in love!" I yelled, suddenly causing a scene as other shoppers stopped and turned to look at us. My mom's eyes widened as my dad took a step back.

"I know you might think you weren't, but we all saw i—"

"It was fake, Mom. The whole thing was fake. Zach and I weren't really dating. We just said that we were."

She shook her head, brows pulled together.

"Why would you do that?" she questioned, her lips pressed together in a thin line.

"Because, Mom," I sighed heavily. "I didn't want you to set

me up with the Hendricks' son. I knew you were pushing me to go because you couldn't stand to see your only daughter still single. So I asked Zach to pretend to be my boyfriend, and things got out of control after that."

My mom lowered her head and took a moment to compose herself.

"I'm sorry, Andi." She looked up at me, her eyes filled with a mixture of tears and disappointment.

"For what?" I asked, confused. I was the one who needed to be sorry.

"For making you think you had to go to the length of having a fake boyfriend just to appease your father and me. All we've ever wanted was for you to be happy, but I never thought it would drive you to this."

I swallowed hard, my throat burning as the tears fought to stay inside.

"No, Mom. I'm sorry. I shouldn't have lied to you guys. I just freaked out, and it seemed like the right thing to do at the time."

My mom stepped closer, brushing her thumb over my cheek.

"My dear, sweet girl. We are proud of you and the life you've created for yourself in Sugarplum Falls. Do we want to see you settle down and find someone to love? Of course. But *true love,* Andi. Like what Zach feels toward you."

I shook my head, refusing to hear what she was saying.

"It wasn't true love, Mom. Yeah, he started having feelings for me, but he wasn't in *love* with me."

"Don't be so sure," she said softly, pulling me in for a hug. "We need to finish our shopping. We're meeting Pearl and Dan for dinner in an hour, and then we're going to see a movie."

"You're still going to hang out with them even though Zach and I aren't really dating?" I asked, surprised that they weren't more bothered by what they just learned.

"Of course we are. They're great people, and your father and I enjoy spending time with them. It's nice to make new friends, and who knows, maybe Sugarplum Falls will be home for us in the future. They're going to take us tomorrow to look at a few houses that recently went up for sale."

"Oh," I stammered. "That's great. It would be nice to have you guys closer."

The hardest part of moving to Sugarplum Falls had been being away from my parents, the only family I had left. Them moving to town would fill a void I had felt ever since I left home.

"Our goal is to be close to our family and friends. Now, take some time to think about things with Zach and stop trying to talk yourself out of it. You've always been the one to stand in your own way."

"Your mom is right, Andi. Zach loves you. It was clear as day to everyone at dinner the other night. You don't have to believe it right now, but at least give it some thought and see if you feel different once you're able to clear your head." My dad smiled softly, a man of little words encouraging his daughter to fall in love with her fake boyfriend.

"There's nothing to think about." I shrugged. I had already accepted that it was over; eventually, they would too.

"Sure there is; you just haven't allowed yourself to get there yet. But you will, trust me." Mom winked and waved before they headed off and left me alone on the aisle.

Twenty-Four
Andi

"Hey, Sam, can I get a—"

"Large peppermint mocha latte with extra whipped cream?" he asked with a grin, finishing my order for me.

"Yes, please," I sighed, sliding my debit card across the counter. "I'm that predictable, aren't I?"

"Not predictable, I just have a knack for remembering people's orders." He smiled warmly and slid my card.

"What would happen if I changed up my order?" I asked playfully.

"I would make it and then try to remember it as an option for next time."

I nodded my head. Sounded easy enough.

"But then I would ask questions to see how you were doing and if anything had changed in your life," he added, catching my eye as he handed my card back.

"Why?"

"Because I know almost everyone's order when they come in. Most of my regulars don't change their coffee orders. They like consistency, they find comfort in their drink, which makes it their go-to. When they ask for something different, I try to figure out what has happened to make them change it. Are they excited about a new job? Did they go through a recent breakup? Have they lost someone they loved? Usually, there's a reason for them getting something different, other than they just wanted something new."

"Oh," I said quietly, suddenly feeling the unease of my feelings about Zach slip through. "That makes sense."

"Take you, for example," he said, turning to talk over his shoulder as he worked on my drink. "If you came in and ordered a salted caramel cold brew instead of your regular drink, I would think it might have something to do with Zach. Maybe something happened between you two, and you wanted something to make you feel closer to him."

I blinked away the tears and rubbed my lips together, my nose burning from trying to hold my emotions together.

Sam gave me a moment and finished my drink before handing it to me. Alongside it were two candy canes. I snorted out a laugh and looked at him. He grinned, his eyes dancing with mischief.

"I have to ask, Sam. What is the deal with the candy canes? I know it's Christmas, so they're part of the season, but why do you give me two every time I order my drink?"

"It's not about the drink," he answered, looking down as he wiped the counter with a rag. Thankfully, it was too early for most people to get up and go on a Tuesday morning, so nobody else was waiting in line.

"What's it about then?"

I vaguely remembered Liv telling me some story, but it still didn't make sense.

"One candy cane is just that, a piece of candy. But two together form a heart. My grandpa believed that they were the key to lover's quarrels. There's nothing that can't be solved over a cup of coffee and something to remind you of the love you have for each other."

A single tear slid down my cheek as I blinked the rest away.

"How do you know so much?"

He shrugged and gave me another smile.

"Some of us have gifts we're meant to share with others. For you, it's those delicious treats you bake with your heart and soul. For me, it's studying people and knowing when to offer advice when I can."

"Thank you, Sam," I said, holding up the candy canes before grabbing my coffee.

I knew Zach would be in soon, and part of me thought it would be nice to welcome him with a cup of coffee like he had done for me so many times. But then the other part of me worried it would send the wrong message by showing I cared for him in a way I hadn't shown before.

Sam grinned wider and lowered his head as if trying to give me privacy while reading the thoughts flooding my mind.

"I'll have a large salted caramel cold brew right up," he answered before I could even ask.

I nodded, my heart racing a mile a minute.

He returned a few minutes later with Zach's drink. I handed him my debit card, but he held his hands up and refused.

"It's on the house."

"Sam, you don't have to do that," I insisted.

"It's my treat. If I don't see you before then, Merry Christmas, Andi."

"Merry Christmas, Sam."

I tucked my chin and headed out, feeling a little lighter than when I went in.

As I walked down the sidewalk back to Sugarplum Sweets, I noticed a giant inflatable elf waving at me. My eyes widened, and my smile spread tightly across my cheeks as I approached Zach while he finished staking it into the patch of grass next to the shop.

"Oh my gosh, this looks amazing!" I squealed, so excited to see it up. Zach had offered to put it up sooner, but between the terrible snowstorm and high winds, there hadn't been a good time before now.

"You like it?" he asked, stepping out from behind the elf.

"I love it. Thank you, Zach."

"You're welcome." He shoved his hands into his pockets and looked down.

"I brought you coffee," I offered, extending his cup to him.

"Thank you. You didn't have to do that."

"You're welcome."

I tried smiling at him but could tell by the way he refused to look at me that he didn't want to see it. I squared my shoulders and tried to force out the rush of rejection that was washing over me. This was what I wanted, so why was I so upset about it?

"Thank you again for putting Elfie up," I said, clearing my throat. "I better get inside and get started on the pastries."

He nodded but said nothing as I walked past him and left the awkwardness that lingered between us out in the frigid air with him.

Twenty-Five
Zach

"Andi won't be there for dinner tomorrow night, Mom," I said sharply, holding the phone between my shoulder and ear as I struggled to wrap the new tackle box for my dad. It was a Friday night, and I was cooped up inside, trying to ignore the heartache I felt.

"But it's Christmas Eve," she pushed. "We just talked about it last weekend before you guys went home. She said she would be there."

I wasn't trying to be grumpy, but it had been three miserable days of working with Andi and acting like nothing had happened. I knew it was what she wanted, but the problem was that we hadn't gone back to how we were *before* we decided to date for pretend. No, it was much worse than that. We acted like two scorned lovers who had really broken up and were forced to figure out how to be around each other. I hated it.

"We can do brunch instead," she offered, not picking up on my tone. Either that, or she was choosing to ignore it.

"No, Mom," I gritted out, slamming the gift down as I tossed the roll of wrapping paper away from me. "Andi won't be there at all because we broke up."

A few seconds of awkwardness passed before she responded. I knew what was coming, which was why I hadn't told her before now that we had broken up. Either that or deep down, a part of me wished Andi would change her mind, and we could skip the whole "break up" drama altogether.

"I know," she sighed.

"You know?"

"Jen told me when we had dinner with them Monday night."

"You went to dinner with her parents?" I asked, surprised by the news.

"And to a movie."

"What?"

"We joined them for a nice dinner at a fancy restaurant and then went to a movie."

"I heard you," I laughed softly, some of the tension releasing. "I just didn't expect to hear that. I was just surprised, that's all."

"We've hung out with them almost every day since then."

"You have?"

"Yes. Your father and I enjoy their company. We actually went with them to look at a few houses in that new neighborhood they're developing. I think they picked one, but they were torn between two. I need to ask her when we see them tonight."

"They're buying a house here?" I asked, ignoring the part about how my parents had a better social life right now than I did.

"They are. They want to be closer to Andi. I think they fell in love with Sugarplum Falls and realized that Andi needs them here as much as they need her."

"Did Jen tell you that…" My voice trailed off as I struggled with how to ask my mom if she knew the whole thing had been fake.

"Tell me what?" she pressed.

"You know. That this whole thing was…"

"Was what?"

I waited a moment, chewing the inside of my lip. I didn't want to admit this to her because it felt like doing so downplayed what I really felt for Andi.

"Fake," I sighed heavily, the words burning my throat.

"Yes."

I leaned against the couch, stretched my legs out in front of me on the rug, and scrubbed a hand down the stubble on my face.

"If you knew, why did you make me say it?" I groaned.

"Because I needed to hear it from you."

"Why?"

"I don't know. I just did."

"Gee, thanks for torturing me two days before Christmas."

"I wasn't trying to torture you," she assured me softly.

"Then what was it?"

"To get confirmation of what I already knew."

"And what's that?"

"That you're head over heels in love with her."

"Yeah, well, that doesn't matter much if she doesn't love me, too," I bit out angrily.

"I wouldn't be so sure she doesn't," she said softly.

"Oh, I'm pretty sure she doesn't. She told me when she insisted on breaking up once she learned I had real feelings for her."

"All I'm saying is stop being stupid and talk to her. Nothing has ever been accomplished by giving someone the silent treatment, you know that."

I sighed heavily into the phone. She was right, even if her words were brutally honest.

"And Zach?"

"Yeah, Mom?"

"I didn't raise a quitter. If you want that girl, you go after her. Show her how much you love her."

"I've tried," I objected before she cut me off.

"SHOW her. Not TELL her. Those are two very different things. I've learned quickly that Andi appreciates acts of kindness. That's how she feels loved. So show her, Zach."

"How am I supposed to do that?" I questioned, scratching my head.

"I don't know. That's not for me to figure out, my love. But I trust you will, and when you do, it'll be worth all of the heartache and sadness you're feeling."

I swallowed hard, wondering what in the world I could do that would show Andi how much she meant to me. I thought I had been doing that already, but apparently, it wasn't enough.

"I've got to get going," my mother said with a sigh. "Call me if you need me. Otherwise, I'll see you both for dinner tomorrow night. Love you."

"Love you too, Mom."

I hung up the phone and rested my head against the couch cushion while I prayed something would come to me.

Twenty-Six
Andi

I sat on my couch Saturday morning, officially off work for a few days as I closed the shop for Christmas Eve and Christmas Day. I knew I would eventually get up and get ready so I could look presentable if my parents stopped by, but now wasn't the time.

I'd barely made it through putting on a cup of coffee and turning the TV on when my doorbell rang. I ran a hand through my hair, hoping to tame the tangled mess I hadn't had a chance to brush yet. Leave it to my parents to show up at nine in the morning on Christmas Eve.

I inhaled slowly and released it as I pulled open the door.

It took my brain a few seconds to register who was on the other side, given that all I could see was a small Christmas tree that hid their face. Once I realized who it was, my heart skipped a beat as I panicked and slammed it shut.

"Can you please open the door, Andi?" Zach asked, his voice sending goosebumps up my skin.

I opened my mouth to say something—anything—but the words refused to come.

"I can't," I lied. "I'm sick."

I pretended to cough, hoping he'd get the message loud and clear.

"Bullshit."

My eyes widened as a smile played on my lips.

"I am sick. Very, very sick. I don't want you to get it."

"Well, lucky for you, I got vaccinated against leptospirosis, so I'm good. I do worry, though, about how often you're interacting with swine."

I shook my head, my arms wrapped around my waist. I wanted to open the door and see him, but I knew my heart wouldn't be able to handle it if I did.

"Now, can you please open the door?" he asked. "It's hard balancing all of this while trying not to spill your peppermint mocha latte from Sugarplum Lattes."

As if knowing the way to my heart, his words had my fingers reaching for the doorknob and turning it to let him inside.

"Thanks," he huffed, brushing past me as he set bags full of stuff on the island along with the tray of drinks.

"What is all of this?" I asked, closing the door before the cold came in.

"This is Christmas Eve." He shrugged, pulled my coffee out, and handed it to me.

"Yes, but why are you here?"

I lifted the cup to my mouth and took a sip. My insides melted, as well as my stress.

"Because you don't have a Christmas tree."

He winked and took a sip of his drink. My eyes fixated on the way his lips brushed against the cup, his mouth parting to take a sip the same way it did when he would kiss me.

"I don't need one," I replied with a shrug.

"Now see, that's where you're wrong." He pointed a finger at me and set his cup down on the island.

"I'm not wrong," I laughed, following him the few feet into my living room as he carried the cute little tree he'd brought with him.

"Yes, Andi. You are. But that's okay because I've come to fix that problem for you."

"By bringing me a tree."

"Exactly."

I shook my head and took another sip. I was going to need more caffeine to follow along and for this to make sense.

"But it's not just any tree, Andi."

"It's not?"

"No," he said, reaching down to plug in the strand of lights attached to it. "It's a tree of love."

"Are you sure? Cause it looks like a plain old Christmas tree to me. Maybe a blue spruce, if I had to guess." I tilted my head and studied it as Zach worked on fluffing out the branches of the artificial tree. Thank God he hadn't gotten me a real one—I would do a terrible job of remembering to water it and keep it from catching on fire.

"It is a blue spruce," he agreed, bending down to reach the lower branches. I looked away to avoid checking out his ass in the jeans he was wearing. They weren't tight, but they stretched perfectly around his body, showing off thick thighs and a plump behind.

"It's also a tree of love," he continued.

"Okay," I said, letting my shoulders fall as I gave in. "What makes it a tree of love? What's so special about it?"

I expected him to tell me some made-up story about it, but instead, he walked away and grabbed a bag from the island. When he returned, he stood before me and looked me in the eye.

"It's not the tree itself that is special, but the love that goes into it. The tree is just a tree. There's nothing special about it. But when you add bits of love to it, then it becomes a tree of love. Just like all of us are fine on our own, but when we start allowing others to love us, it makes it easier for us to give our love as well."

I swallowed hard, having an idea where this was going.

Zach reached in and pulled out an ornament, handing it to me.

"Zach," I gasped, holding my hand over my mouth. "It's gorgeous!"

"That one is from your parents."

He smiled as I studied the delicate wood ornament in my hands. It was a circle with a woman wearing an apron and holding a rolling pin that had my name engraved on it. Around the outside of the circle it read: life is what you bake of it.

"My parents?" I asked, turning it around to admire it.

"They went to Wes's shop this morning and asked if he could do a custom order."

"But he's been busy for weeks," I said quietly. "I've heard people complaining that they didn't get their orders in on time.

"Yeah, but you know small-town magic—there's always a little left right before Christmas. When we told Wes what we were doing, he was happy to do it. He also made this one specifically for you."

He handed me another wooden ornament, this one a Christmas tree with a star on top and my name written in the middle.

"He knew it was your first Christmas tree and wanted to make sure you had the perfect keepsake to remember it," he explained. "Go ahead and put them on the tree." He nodded, giving me time to soak up the moment.

I gently placed both ornaments on the tree and stepped back to look at it. My heart felt larger already.

"This one is from Liv," he said, pulling another ornament out of the bag. "She has the other half on her tree at home."

I grinned when I saw that it was a heart broken in half with *best friends* written across it. Although my half only said: be fri. But I knew it had to be adorable when put together. I reached over and hung it on the tree while Zach pulled the next ornament out and waited for me.

"This is from my parents."

He handed me a silver-shaped star ornament that had gold glitter across the front of it. He flipped it over, and I noticed the message written on the back.

Andi,

You're such a shining star in our lives!

Pearl & Dan

My eyes welled with tears as I hung it on the branch. I wiped them away with the backs of my hands, thankful he didn't bother to mention it.

We went on for a few minutes as he handed me ornament after ornament, each one with a different note from someone in town who wanted to shower me with some *tree love*. I couldn't believe that he had pulled this off in such a short amount of time or that he had thought to do it, to begin with.

Finally, we got to the end of the bag with just a few ornaments remaining.

He pulled out a heart candy cane one, and I grinned.

"Sam?" I asked, taking it from his fingers.

He nodded.

"He said you already know the story, so he wanted you to have a reminder when you needed it," Zach explained before pulling two actual candy canes out of the bag. "These also came with our order this morning."

I laughed and took them from him, adding them to the tree as well, trying to get them as close to a heart shape as possible.

Zach fidgeted with the bag for a moment as he retrieved the final one. My heart started to speed up as I noticed how anxious he suddenly became. I assumed the last ornament was from him, but the way he was acting had my nerves going crazy, too.

The first one he handed me was a ceramic ornament with a girl soaking in a bath overflowing with bubbles and a glass of wine in her hand.

"Thank you, Zach," I said softly, holding it close to my chest. "I love it."

His cheeks flushed a little bit as he held out his fist and waited for me to open his fingers to see what was inside. I eyed him suspiciously as I did, making sure I didn't drop the ornament.

A silver key sparkled in his hand, the lights from the Christmas tree reflecting off it.

I pinched my brows together, unsure of why he was giving me a key.

"Move in with me, Andi," he blurted out.

My eyes widened as my eyebrows shot up my forehead.

"What?" I gasped, clearly having heard him wrong.

"Move in with me."

"I… Um." I stepped back and shook my head, refusing to touch the key that was still resting in the palm of his hand.

I sat down on the couch, too puzzled to speak. The cushion shifted as he sat beside me.

"I know you're scared, Andi. I am, too. I wasn't supposed to fall for my boss, but here we are. And I won't apologize for it because you're the greatest thing that has ever happened to me. I know you don't think this thing between us can work, but I disagree. I'll go to my grave using my last breath to tell you how much I love you, Andi. And whatever the reason is for you not wanting us to be together, we'll work through it because I would rather fight with you every day about us being together than risk you going one single day not knowing how I feel about you."

"Zach, I," I breathed out, but my words got lodged in my throat.

"I know you're looking for a reason why this *can't* work out between us, but all I'm focused on are the reasons why it *can.* There's a chemistry there that you can't deny. I've felt it, and I know you did, too. But trust me when I say that I will take this however slow you want to take it. You don't have to move in with me today—though I have my truck, so if you say yes and want to, I can also make that happen." He winked. "I'm just saying that I'm not going anywhere, Andi. No matter how hard I have to work to get you to love me back, I'll do it."

The tears ran down my face as I lowered my head to keep from looking at him.

"I don't want to give up my shop," I said quietly, in between sniffles.

"Who's asking you to?"

He leaned over and lifted my chin with his finger.

"If it comes down to you loving me or you working with me, and you *have* to choose one—I'll find another job on Monday. I don't care, Andi. I love my job and spending time with you at Sugarplum Sweets, but I won't jeopardize having a chance at *forever* with you."

"My ex made me choose between him and my work. He didn't understand how I could love something so much, and it wasn't him. I don't want that guilt again, Zach. I don't want to have to explain why I'm working late or be accused of cheating because I'm spending long hours at the shop."

"First of all, I would never do that to you. I want you to chase your dreams, baby. I want to lift you onto my shoulders just to get you a little closer to reaching them. I want to push you to do whatever makes you happy and be there alongside you as we do this together."

"I don't know how to do all of this," I admitted, wiping my tears away again. "I've never been in love before, and the only time I thought I was, it ended really bad. That was when I decided to move away and start over. I've worked my ass off to get to where I am."

"And like I said, I'm not going to do anything to jeopardize that, Andi. It's okay to let your guard down with me. This is a safe place, and no one is going to take what you've built for yourself away. I promise."

I inhaled deeply, allowing the oxygen to flush through my body as I calmly let it out.

"Are we crazy for rushing into this, though?" I asked, chewing my nails nervously.

"I don't think there's much we're rushing," he said with a shrug. "We've already had sex and pretended to date, so that's covered. And you've stayed at my house a handful of times, so it's not like you're uncomfortable there. I love you. I *think* you love me, too. Plus, I have the soaking tub you really lo—"

"Sold," I interrupted, laughing at the hurt look on his face before I pulled him into me and kissed him.

"Are you just using me for my tub?" he teased, his mouth still pressed tightly against mine.

"Maybe."

Twenty-Seven
Zach

I spent the morning at Andi's, helping her decorate a tree that would be moving to my house soon. I still couldn't believe she had agreed to move in with me. Things were clearer now that we had talked, and I understood better where she was coming from as far as why she didn't want to be in a relationship. She opened up more, and I found myself wanting to find her ex so I could wring his neck for putting her through all that.

We got to my house a little after one, stopping to grab some takeout from the only Chinese food place open in Sugarplum Falls today.

"Have you decided what you're going to wear tonight?" I asked, popping the last bite of eggroll into my mouth and crumpling the wrapper.

"No, have you?"

I shook my head, still feeling over the moon that she was sitting in my kitchen and talking about what to wear to dinner at my parents' tonight.

"I'm surprised your mom wanted to do another themed party," Andi said behind her napkin as she chewed. "I thought only the Hendricks were that obsessed with themed parties."

"I told you, she loves parties and will throw one any chance she gets."

Andi tilted her head and studied me for a moment.

"Does she not always do a themed party for Christmas Eve?"

"Nope. Usually, we just wear whatever and hang out."

"So what's so special about this year?"

"You."

I smiled at the way her skin flushed pink around her cheeks.

"Oh, stop it," she giggled as I stood up to throw my trash away and tickled her sides on my way to the trashcan.

"It's true," I said as she grabbed hers and joined me.

I held the lid open as she tossed her empty plate and napkin, then pulled her into my arms and held her.

"I hardly believe I'm the reason to have such an elaborate party."

"Of course you are. My parents are thrilled that I'm bringing a girl to dinner."

"Yeah, but you've taken someone before. Haven't you?"

I shook my head.

"Oh. I thought your mom was just being nice when she said you've never done that before."

I pulled her tighter and kissed her forehead.

"It was the truth. I've never brought anyone home to meet them and definitely never had a date for Christmas Eve dinner."

"Wow." She pulled her shoulders back and looked at me. "I feel so special."

"You are. Now, let's go pick what we're wearing so I can ravish you a few times before we have to go."

I growled and nipped her ear before she pulled away and went running down the hall to my bedroom. *Our bedroom.*

Twenty-Eight
Andi

"Hey, can you help me get the zipper up the rest of the way?" I asked, standing in the entryway as I pushed the earring through my ear and secured the back.

"Nope, I can't." Zach stood behind me, his hands slowly roaming over my hips before dipping to my front, trying to make their way to the promised land. "But I *can* help take this off."

"Zach," I laughed, pulling away. We had to leave in less than ten minutes, and there was no way I was going to show up at his parents' house—with MY parents there—wearing wet panties.

"THIS is the dress you picked for tonight?" he growled, moving my hair to the side as his fingers brushed against my skin, working the zipper. I tilted my head, allowing the soft curls to fall to the side.

"Your mom said *little black dress* was fine when I texted her to ask for confirmation."

"I don't think she meant *this* little." His fingers continued to caress my skin as he pulled the zipper down and then brushed against the hem of my dress.

"It's not that short."

"Your legs look insane in it," he grumbled.

"That's just from the heels I'm wearing."

"You're trying to kill me."

I turned around and faced him, cupping the material against my chest before the dress fell to the floor.

"No, I'm not," I laughed. "Now, please hurry up and zip me, or we're going to be late."

"Fine," he groaned, spinning me around so he could pull it up.

"Done."

"Thank you. Now that wasn't so hard, was it?" I teased, grabbing the bracelet I'd set on the entryway table and fastening it on my wrist.

He stepped away, his eyes fixated on my body as he drank me in. I could feel the heat rush through me and tried to remind myself that we didn't have time for this right now.

"Oh, and Andi?"

I stopped what I was doing and looked up at him.

My name on his lips caught me off guard as he leaned against the wall, one foot crossed over the other, making his pressed slacks and dark button-down shirt scream for me to remove them. My eyes traveled down to the prominent bulge, wetting my lips as I licked them.

"Yeah?" I whispered, unable to get my voice louder.

"Just so you know, you'll be riding my face while wearing that later."

My jaw dropped as I stood there, wondering if it was too late to take him up on that offer now.

"We better get going," he said, pushing off the wall and placing a hand on my lower back to guide me.

"Okay," I replied, shaking my head to clear the lust-induced fog. "Just one second."

I gripped his bicep, steadying myself as I reached under my dress, pulled the black lace panties down my legs, and tossed them to the couch behind us.

"What are you doing?" he asked, his voice low.

"It would be rude to show up with wet panties," I replied, batting my eyes innocently at him. "Besides, I figured you'd appreciate the *fast food* when we got home."

He closed his eyes and groaned as I grabbed my purse from the table and sauntered out the door ahead of him. Tonight was going to be a long, *hard* night.

By the time we got to his parents' house, I had been able to get all of the dirty, naughty things I wanted to do to their son out of my head. Sure, I had been forced to think about the stock market crashing and quadratic equations to do so, but at least I wasn't on the verge of jumping his bones in front of everyone.

Pearl was already at the door when we got there, saying hello to my parents, who had been invited as well. It still felt odd how quickly our parents had become best friends, but I didn't mind it one bit. It was nice to see my parents so happy, and I couldn't remember the last time my mom had another woman to hang out with.

"Oh, Andi, you look beautiful," Pearl said, pulling me in for a cheek kiss so we didn't smear each other's makeup.

"Thank you. You look amazing. That purple really makes your eyes pop," I commented, genuinely meaning what I said.

Her dress was a floor-length velvet material that hugged her curves and left a little bit of cleavage on display with the v-neckline. I couldn't see what shoes she was wearing, but it sounded like heels as we walked across the tile entryway into the house.

My mother had on a satin red dress that I had seen once before when she and my father went to a Broadway show. She looked amazing, and I loved how my dad had matched her with his red striped tie.

"Dinner smells amazing," Zach said, greeting everyone with hugs.

"Thank you. It's just about ready," Pearl replied, grinning as she led everyone to the dining room.

I stopped for a moment to take in the beautiful centerpieces with fresh flowers and candles centered on the sides of the vases to create the perfect ambiance. Wine glasses were already filled, and each seat had a personal place setting with a notecard sitting on top of the plates.

I found mine and sat down, not surprised that I was tucked in between Zach and my dad.

"Go ahead and read the cards," Pearl said, setting the last dish on the table as Dan helped with the others.

They sat and joined us, everyone opening the envelopes to read what was inside.

My eyes watered as I studied the cursive words written in black ink:

You are the best gift any of us could ask for

I looked up to find Pearl watching me, her cheeks dimpled from her grin and hands folded in front of her. I mouthed *thank you* and then leaned into Zach.

"What does yours say?" he asked, kissing my forehead for what felt like the millionth time since he'd come by my apartment this morning.

"It says I'm the best gift they could have asked for," I replied, my heart still swelling with pride. "What does yours say?"

"I told you to stop being stupid with a smiley face at the end."

"Yeah, right," I laughed, rolling my eyes. "What does it really say?"

He grinned and turned his card so I could read it.

I told you to stop being stupid :-)

"Oh my gosh," I giggled, holding my hands to cover my face.

"Before we start eating, I want to make a toast," Daniel said, lifting his glass.

We all quieted down and lifted ours as we gave him our attention.

"To friends that have quickly turned into family. Pearl and I are so happy to welcome you into our home this holiday season and into our hearts forever. Merry Christmas."

"Merry Christmas," I said softly, clinking my glass with those around me.

We all took a sip and then began eating while our parents dove right into conversation.

Twenty-Nine
Zach

Four hours, twenty-seven minutes, and eighteen seconds—that was how long I had to wait until we got home and I got between Andi's legs.

Since she'd decided to go commando to the party, I thought it was only fair to tease her on the way home by playing with her beautiful little pussy while I drove. She was soaking wet, her lips glistening with arousal by the time I parked and carried her in over my shoulder, holding down her dress so my neighbors didn't see anything.

"I've been waiting a while for this," I growled, loosening my tie as she stood in the living room, chewing her nail as she watched me.

"Is that so?"

"I don't joke when it comes to eating your pussy, Andi."

"Hmm. And here I thought you got enough to eat at dinner." She tapped her chin playfully while pretending to think about it.

"I told you I was eating this when we got home, and I meant it. You're going to hike up that little dress and ride my face until you come."

Something flashed across her face, and she tried to look away before I noticed, but it was too late.

"What was that look about?" I asked softly, grabbing her arm and pulling her into me.

"Nothing," she lied, looking everywhere but at me.

"Bullshit. Tell me, Andi."

"It's nothing, I promise."

"No, there was a look that flashed across your face, and I want to know what it was."

"That's my turned-on face," she said with a shrug.

"Andi, you better start talking or so help me, God…"

I shook my head and looked up at the ceiling.

"Or what? What are you going to do?" she asked playfully, poking her finger into my chest.

I knew this was just her way of changing the subject, but I wasn't ready to do so just yet.

"I'm going to bend you over my knee while you're still wearing this dress and spank that ass hard enough that your pussy aches to be fucked."

She licked her lips, slowly nodding as if she were on board with this plan.

"Then I'm going to rub your clit until you com—"

Just then, that same look flashed across her face, the color draining from it when she realized that I had just figured it out.

I inhaled deeply and worked my jaw as I tried to figure out what to say.

"Is that the problem? Do you not like coming?" I asked softly, folding my arms over my chest to keep from touching her right now. We needed to have an open, honest conversation without lust getting in the way.

"It's not that," she whispered, looking at the ground. "Sex with you is great. I enjoy it."

"I didn't ask about sex. I asked about coming. Do you not like it?" I repeated, keeping any hint of frustration out of my voice. I just wanted answers. "Is that why you faked it with me?"

She shook her head but refused to look at me.

"If we're going to do this and be in a relationship, we have to be able to talk to each other, Andi. About everything."

"It's not a big deal." She shrugged.

"It is to me. If you don't like it, I won't try to make you come. But I need to know what's going on and what your boundaries are. That's very important to me."

"I can't."

Her words were so quiet I almost missed them.

"You can't tell me?" I pressed.

"No, I can't have an orgasm."

I pressed my lips together to keep from overwhelming her with the million questions that were rushing through my head.

"Like it's medically impossible?" I asked.

She shook her head and then finally looked at me.

"I don't know. Maybe? I've never gone to a doctor about it."

"Okay," I said softly. "Then what makes you think you *can't?*"

She shrugged and let her shoulders fall heavily, the thin strap of her dress sliding down her arm. I reached over and slid it back into place, so I didn't get distracted.

"My ex used to say it was impossible. And the few guys I dated after that."

I worked my jaw, trying to get past the jealousy I felt from another man touching her.

"How often did they try?" I asked, hating the way the words tasted on my tongue.

"Once or twice. They didn't bother much after that. I was always told that I took too long and that they would try again later, but they never did. My last ex was the one who told me it was a *me* problem and insisted he could get any woman off. I don't know why, but I believed him. That thought just rooted itself in my mind."

I closed my eyes and pulled in a deep, calming breath. The guys she had been with were idiots—there was no doubt about that.

"Have you ever tried to get yourself off?" I asked softly, shifting the attention away from those losers and back to her.

"No."

"Why not? If you don't mind me asking. I don't want to make you uncomfortable."

"I don't know," she sighed heavily, sitting on the arm of the couch. "Sex and stuff related to it were never talked about much while I was growing up and I guess I never had anyone I felt comfortable going to for advice. I didn't have those girl friends that sat around comparing stories and sharing tips, so to speak."

I stepped closer, closing the space between us. She looked away as if embarrassed to admit this to me. But I didn't want her to feel that way at all. I wanted her to know she could trust me with anything she said.

"Andi," I said softly, lifting her from the couch by her elbow until she stood in front of me. "Thank you for telling me. It means a lot to me that you did."

She nodded and tried to smile, but it fell flat against her lips.

"Now that we have that covered, I still want you to ride my face. You don't have to stress about whether or not you come. I just want you to enjoy it. And if you ever want to explore and try new things to get you to orgasm, I'm 1000% on board with that."

"You sound quite confident you can get me there," she teased, her body not as stiff against mine as it was a few minutes ago.

"Oh, trust me—I know the way to a woman's heart," I said, reaching down to grab her hand and then leading her to the bedroom.

"But I thought you said you were going to make me come?"

"I am."

"But the way to a woman's heart—"

"Is through her clit, Andi. Let's go."

Thirty
Andi

"You remember Candy Cane," Zach said, pulling out the red and white striped vibrator and handing it to me. "I've already cleaned it and put batteries in it so you can go through the different modes and see which one you want to try."

"Modes?" I questioned with a raised eyebrow as I took it.

"Yeah, different speeds. Different pulses. Just push the power button to go through each one."

I eyed him suspiciously as I did what he asked. I held the power button down for a few seconds until the toy came to life, vibrating softly as I held it in my hand. I pressed it again and the vibration got stronger. My eyes widened when I pushed it a third time, and it increased even more.

I kept going, curious to see what all it could do. It vibrated, then stopped, and just as I was going to tell Zach that it was broken, it started up again.

"Different pulses," he answered, reading my mind.

It wasn't bad, though I couldn't say whether or not I would like it down there. As I continued, the pulses either got stronger or quicker.

"What the heck is this?" I asked Zach, holding up the vibrator as it buzzed in the air. "Is this like some sort of

SOS signal? Is this for a pussy in distress?" I shook my head, trying not to laugh at the vibrator as it spelled some sort of unknown code against my hand, going between short and long pulses.

"I think it is," he said, coming around to the side of the bed I was sitting on. "I definitely heard her call out for help. Don't worry, I know pussy CPR."

His eyes lit up as he gently pushed me back onto the pillows and took the vibrator from my hands. He climbed up the bed, spreading my legs as my dress lifted higher, showing him my freshly shaved pussy.

"She's ready for mouth-to-mouth," I teased, giggling as he grabbed my hips and pulled me down.

Within seconds, his mouth was over my wetness, tongue sliding deep inside me.

I arched my back and allowed myself to be in the moment without having to worry about faking anything. I wasn't expecting to have an orgasm—especially since I had never had one before in my life—but that didn't mean I didn't enjoy the way Zach made my body feel.

I moaned and dug my fingers into the sheets until Zach pulled away and looked into my eyes.

"I wasn't kidding when I said I wanted you to ride my face, Andi. It can be my Christmas gift," he said, wiggling his eyebrows.

I pulled my lower lip between my teeth as I considered it.

"Well, I guess the actual gift I bought you is no good now," I teased as he laid beside me and held his hand out for me to take it.

I rolled over, straddling his stomach as his hands gripped my hips and held me steady. Then, with a glimmer in his eye, he slid down and disappeared under the skirt of my dress.

The thought of riding his face was so arousing that I felt my wetness drip down the insides of my thighs as he began slow, torturous licks along my slit. I spread my legs further, allowing him more access as I rocked gently back and forth.

I could feel the heat spread throughout my body as it reacted to his touch, to his lips as they kissed my lips, and to his finger as it slid inside.

"Ahhhh," I cried out, sinking lower over his mouth.

His finger curled deeper inside me, pressing against a spot that threatened to make me see stars with the pressure he was putting on it.

"Zach," I panted, rubbing against him though not knowing what I needed. "Make me come. Please."

Without saying a word, he flipped me onto my back and lay beside me as his finger continued to fuck me. Then he locked his leg over mine, keeping it in place as he started rubbing my clit with his middle finger.

"Fuck, Andi," he moaned, kissing the side of my neck. "You're so fucking wet."

His dirty words sent a jolt of electricity through me. I could feel my spine tingle and waves of heat rush through me as I held my breath.

"Breathe through it, baby. Deep, quick breaths," he coaxed, lowering the top of my dress before kissing my breasts.

I did as he said, focusing on the build-up, though I didn't know what to do with it.

He continued rubbing my clit, but I could tell that he noticed when I started to pull my legs together.

"You take my cock so good, Andi," he said, freeing a nipple from the lace bra I was wearing and sucking it between his teeth. "And the way you suck my dick, ooh baby, you drive me wild. I love how your mouth works me so good until you swallow my cum down that tight little throat of yours."

"Mmmm," I moaned, even more aroused by his words.

"And these fucking tits, I could drive my cock right between them, fucking your tits until I come all over your chest. Would you like that, baby? Or would you rather suck me dry?"

"I want you to come on my chest," I answered, my body on fire as it reacted to his touch.

He rubbed harder against my clit, keeping the same motion and speed as before.

"I want to sit you on the table at work and eat your pussy until you come, Andi," he continued. "I'd make everyone watch as I claimed what was mine, making sure they all knew whose name you were calling out when you touched yourself at your desk."

I tossed my head back and arched my back, the thought of it too arousing.

"You're going to do that for me, aren't you, baby? Sit in your office, pretending to work while you finger this tight pussy, imagining it's me under your desk, eating you out. Oh, God, Andi, the amount of times that you'll come just from thinking about all the places I'm going to fuck you at work."

The pressure increased from his fingers at the same time I felt pressure increasing down there. He rubbed harder and faster as I panted and listened to the filthy words he spoke.

"FUCK!" I cried out, my hips bucking off the bed as he held me down and continued to draw my very first orgasm out of me.

Waves of pleasure rocked me, sending jolt after jolt of electricity through my body until my skin was too sensitive to touch.

Zach slowly pulled his hand away and kissed my temple as he lay on his back beside me.

"That was…" I stalled, unable to think of the right words. "Incredible."

"We're only getting started, baby," he said, kissing me.

I turned my head to look at him, feeling something shift inside of me as soon as he turned to look at me. It was then that I knew I was madly, deeply in love with this man.

"I love you," I whispered, curling into his chest as I closed my eyes and let him hold me.

BLAME IT ON THE CANDY CANES

Thirty-One
Andi

"Merry Christmas," Zach whispered in my ear, planting kisses along my neck as he woke me up.

"Merry Christmas," I said groggily, struggling to wake up as I rolled onto my back, my breasts exposed as the sheet slipped down.

Zach pulled it further and then leaned in and pulled a pebbled nipple into his mouth. The combination of the cold air in the room combined with the warmth from his tongue was driving me crazy.

His hand slipped between my thighs, rubbing along my slit before pushing a finger inside. I gasped softly at the welcomed intrusion and opened my legs wider for him. We spent the night last night playing a game called *Guess how many times Andi can come.* The record had been seven times in six hours, but he was determined to beat that today.

I reached over and grabbed his cock, not at all surprised that he was already hard for me. I stroked gently, teasing with tugs here and there that earned a deep growl in my ear every time I played with his balls.

"Did she miss me?" he asked, removing his fingers for a second to grab the vibrator from the nightstand.

"Mmm hmm," I moaned, spreading them wider as he pushed the button and turned it on. "She needs her fill of you this morning."

"Oh, trust me, baby, I'm about to fill her up real good."

He pressed the tip of the vibrator against my clit and chuckled when my body bucked against his hand. Then he inserted the long part of the candy cane inside me, fucking me with it slowly while the curved head of it rested perfectly against my clit.

Now that I had come a few times, I recognized the signs quickly and got myself ready for another mind-blowing orgasm. Zach pushed it deeper, sucking my nipples harder as I scratched my nails into the sheets to gain purchase as he increased the speed and intensity of the vibrator.

Within seconds, I was screaming his name as waves of pleasure rolled over me.

"That's my girl, coming so good on that toy," he praised, turning it off and tossing it to the side so we could clean it later.

He lined himself up at my entrance and gave me a second before sliding inside and fucking me the way I needed to be fucked.

We didn't last as long as we did last night, probably because we were both exhausted from the lack of sleep. But neither of us complained as he unloaded inside me, his orgasm bringing on another of my own as his cock constantly rubbed my clit.

Once we were done, we cleaned up in the shower and threw on pajamas until we had to head to my parent's rental for dinner. It turned out they had made an offer on it, and it was no longer just a rental for them. It still blew my mind that they were moving to Sugarplum Falls and that I would be able to see them whenever I wanted.

"Do you want coffee?" Zach asked as we headed into the kitchen. "It's not as good as Sam's, but it's not bad either."

"Sure, that sounds great. Thank you."

He gave me a kiss as he passed by me to get the coffee started.

"Do you want me to make something for breakfast?" I offered, feeling unsure of what to do. I was going to be living here soon, but that didn't mean I was used to it yet.

"I can cook if you tell me what you want. Or, we can open presents and eat when we're done," he offered, a mischievous grin on his face.

"Definitely presents," I said with a laugh. "I'm curious to see what that smile is all about."

We went to the living room while the coffee brewed and sat by the tree that was loaded with wrapped presents beneath it. Most of them were to take to my parent's house later, including some for his parents as well. I had brought everything I had from home, thankful I had thought ahead to buy gifts for Zach without knowing we would be together.

"You first," he said, handing me a garment-sized box wrapped in silver paper with a red bow.

I ripped it open and laughed when I found an apron inside with the words "Master Baker" written on the front with a rolling pin and oven mitt. Beneath it was another apron.

"That one is for me," he informed me with a toothy smile.

I pulled it out and held it up, laughing when I read "Masturbater" on it.

"Oh my gosh! Zach!" I shrieked, giggling as I tossed it at him.

"What can I say?" He shrugged. "It's what I do best."

"Well, in that case, I'm going to need proof," I teased, not remembering who I was dealing with.

His eyebrows raised in challenge as he reached a hand into his joggers and started to pull his cock out.

"Not right now." I laughed harder. "Open my gift first."

He kept his hand on his dick for a moment longer, watching as I struggled to keep my eyes on his face.

I grabbed the gift I wanted him to open, stopping for a moment when I noticed something on the tree. My fingers reached up and gently touched the heart frame ornament he got in the exchange at his parents. Inside was the selfie we had taken before we went in at the Hendrick's party in the truck.

"Zach," I said quietly, my throat tight as I held back my emotions. "It's beautiful."

"Thank you. I told you I had the perfect picture for it."

"But it doesn't match the snowflakes," I commented, still staring at the beautiful ornament I was holding.

"No, but it's better."

I pressed my lips together and tried to blink away the tears as he opened his gift from me.

"Thank you so much, Andi. These are perfect," he said, holding up the molds I had bought for the truffles he loved to make. I knew he loved to work with his hands instead of using molds, but these were shaped as different ornaments and reminded me of Zach.

We continued opening presents, then ate and rested before we had to get ready to go to my parents' house for dinner. It still felt surreal that everything I thought I could ever want in life was actually happening.

While I thought it would be awkward dating Zach since we worked together, I realized these past few weeks that no one cared. There wasn't the gossip I had anticipated, and it turned out everyone had been expecting us to get together all along, given the chemistry they had seen between us.

I didn't know what the future held, but as long as Zach was in it, that was all that mattered.

****

Looking for more steamy holiday romance? Be sure to check these novellas out!

Grab your FREE copy of A Very Merry Kissmas here: https://BookHip.com/MCQQZTS

Sugarplum Falls Series:

Blame It On The Mistletoe

https://books2read.com/u/bw1rqe

Blame It On The Eggnog

https://books2read.com/u/38PPY6

Standalones:

Snow Place To Go

https://books2read.com/u/4A560N

A Christmas Wish

https://books2read.com/u/4EKXpE

Holiday Hijinks

https://books2read.com/u/4DP6Ze

Other Books By Samantha Baca

The Haven Brook Series
(small-town romantic suspense):

'Til Death Do Us Part (Haven Brook Book 1)

https://books2read.com/u/m2RJNR

The Cradle Will Fall (Haven Brook Book 2)

https://books2read.com/u/b6O0QE

The Ties That Bind (Haven Brook Book 3)

https://books2read.com/u/mqgoz8

A Very Haven Christmas (Haven Brook Book 4- Novella)

https://books2read.com/u/mvqGjj

Three Strikes, You're Gone (Haven Brook Book 5)

https://books2read.com/u/mvqL2z

The Dark Shadows Trilogy
(romantic suspense)

Five Steps Ahead (Dark Shadows Book 1)

https://books2read.com/u/38Q0gO

Ten Seconds Too Late (Dark Shadows Book 2)

https://books2read.com/u/3JRgVB

Against The Clock (Dark Shadows Book 3)

https://books2read.com/u/m2YwoR

The Stone Creek Series
(small-town- novellas)

Chocolate Covered Mistletoe (Stone Creek Book 1)

https://books2read.com/u/3LRk9N

Candy Coated Promises (Stone Creek Book 2)

https://books2read.com/u/mldP5Y

Pumpkin Spiced Possibilities (Stone Creek Book 3)

https://books2read.com/u/bojdwV

Beaumont Creek Series
(small town)

Just One Time (Beaumont Creek Book 1)

https://books2read.com/u/3G52zK

Second Chances (Beaumont Creek Book 2)

https://books2read.com/u/4Aj6Z0

Third Time's The Charm (Beaumont Creek Book 3)

https://books2read.com/u/b5lEyG

Four-ever Single (Beaumont Creek Book 4)

https://books2read.com/u/4j5jMX

Fifth Wheel (Beaumont Creek Book 5)

https://books2read.com/u/4XwKwa

Whiskey Mountain Series (small-town- novellas)

Something To Talk About

https://books2read.com/u/4X62ag

Something To Think About

https://books2read.com/u/3GWAan

Something To Believe In

https://books2read.com/u/3yVzgB

Something To Live For

https://books2read.com/u/mllEOP

<u>Sugarplum Falls Series</u>
<u>(Holiday Novellas- can be read as standalone)</u>

Blame It On The Mistletoe

https://books2read.com/u/bw1rqe

Blame It On The Eggnog

https://books2read.com/u/38PPY6

Blame It On The Candy Canes

https://books2read.com/u/31DNo7

Blame It On The Blizzard

https://books2read.com/u/b6z6XE

<u>Standalone Books</u>

One Last Wish

https://books2read.com/u/mqg7D9

Finding Love In Apartment 2C (novella)

https://books2read.com/u/bze9aZ

Cocky Counsel: A Hero Club Novel

https://books2read.com/u/31Kzkn

All Is Fair In Food And War (novella)

https://books2read.com/u/bp8qjX

<u>Holiday Books</u>

<u>(novellas)</u>

Snow Place To Go

https://books2read.com/u/4A560N

A Christmas Wish

https://books2read.com/u/4EKXpE

Holiday Hijinks

https://books2read.com/u/4DP6Ze

Acknowledgments

As always, I want to start by saying thank you to every single person who picked up this book and read it. I know you have hundreds of options, and I'm honored that you selected mine. Thank you so much!

I couldn't do this without the support and guidance of my alpha and beta readers. Thank you, Amanda. You're always there whether I need feedback on the book or just a smile on my face. I appreciate you and our friendship, even if I've thanked you for what feels like the hundredth time. I'll never stop bragging about how good you are to me!

Claire, Jackie, Valerie, and Malissa—I'm so lucky to have the best beta readers in the world! You ladies are quick to find plot holes, as well as those pesky errors that we miss in the first few rounds of editing. Your feedback is greatly appreciated, and I'm so happy to have you on my team.

My parents and sister will always be part of my biggest support team, along with my hubby and sweet girls. I couldn't do this without the love and devotion you all have for making my dreams come true. I love you all!

To the ARC readers, bloggers, Instagrammers, and Booktokers who have so selflessly helped promote my book, thank you so much! You're such an essential part of this process, and I'm so thankful for you!

About the Author

Samantha lives in the southwest with her husband and two small children after abandoning her childhood dream of living in a cabin in Colorado when she found that she couldn't afford to live there and was deathly allergic to the woods. When she's not writing, she's usually spouting off sarcastic remarks while drinking wine out of a coffee mug to look like a functional adult while chasing down her toddlers. She enjoys spending time with her family, watching reruns of Friends, and the 24/7 flow of coffee that can be found in her veins. Be sure to follow her on social media for updates on what she's working on.

You can find her here:

Facebook: https://www.facebook.com/AuthorSamanthaBaca

Instagram: https://instagram.com/author_samantha_baca

Goodreads: http://www.goodreads.com/authorsamanthabaca

Facebook Reader Group:https://www.facebook.com/groups/2945710968775398/

Webpage: https://authorsamanthabaca.wordpress.com

Newsletter: http://eepurl.com/g0NcSj

www.ingramcontent.com/pod-product-compliance
Lightning Source LLC
Chambersburg PA
CBHW061529310726
48972CB00008B/2374